of

Forgotten Lives

By Brian W Taylor

Congratulations.

I hope you enjoy the book.

Brian Taylor

CHAPTER ONE

The grounds of Moorecroft House weren't haunted. They *weren't* haunted. I'd been telling myself that every moment since, as new boy on the gardening staff, I'd been set to work on my own with a pair of powered hedge cutters, trimming the hedge along the haunted track the Grey Lady was said to race along from time to time, screaming for her husband to take pity on her and save her from the executioner's axe. It was a bit disconcerting, then, when, on my first morning there, concern about the possibility of the Grey Lady appearing through the mist along the haunted ride had been superseded by a more immediate concern about a small, dark haired man, dressed in Elizabethan doublet and hose, holding a hat with a feather in one hand, and a corncob pipe in the other, who had suddenly appeared out of the mists along the haunted path as I stood back, cutters in hand, to admire my handiwork with the yew hedge, and now stood watching me with what seemed to my fevered imagination to be demonic intensity.

"Have you got a light?"

I jumped involuntarily. "What?" Whatever I had expected the apparition to say, it wasn't that.

"Have you got a light?" He waved the corncob pipe in front of me. "For the pipe."

"No," I answered briefly, my work in abeyance for the moment, still not sure what to make of him. "Sorry. I don't smoke."

"Oh." He shook his head sadly at that. "Not enough people do these days."

"I don't do drugs either." I spoke sharply, holding the hedge cutters in front of me like a barrier I hoped would keep him at bay if he'd intended violence of some sort towards me. "If you were hoping for a fix." I don't know why I said it, except that the look of him was so unusual I thought he might be one of the junkies I'd also been warned I might encounter out in the woods.

He seemed completely unphased about getting the answer to a question he hadn't asked me. "Too many people do that these days." He frowned, put the pipe away in his pocket, and then looked at me with smiling eyes. "First day here?"

"Yes," I admitted.

"Thought I was a ghost, didn't you?" He laughed loudly.

"No!" I replied indignantly. Then, more honestly. "Well, yes, I did actually. Appearing out of the mist behind me like that."

"I should have thought. I suppose no one told you some of us have to be in costume?"

"Us?" I looked back at him blankly and his smile grew a little broader. "Costume?"

"Us tour guides. We have to dress up for the period we're dealing with when we're in front of the public. Today it's Tudor England, so I'm dressed for the time of Henry VIII. Tomorrow it might be Victorian England. I'm Geoff Truscott, by the way." He held out a hand by way of greeting." Oh don't worry about that!" As I looked at my own dirty hands dubiously, and wiped them on the front of my shirt before I took his. "I've been unblocking toilets with mine. I'm joking." He said as I took my own hand back quickly. "I'm always joking. When you've been here longer you'll know that."

Moorecroft House, where we were both working, was a mansion situated to the north of Church Stretton in Shropshire, and dating from the beginning of the eighteenth century. The original building, from which the first Lady Moorecroft, the one who was supposed to haunt the grounds as the Grey Lady, having committed a gross act of folly by seducing a young troubadour her husband had employed to entertain her in other ways, was taken one morning to be executed in the local market town, had been burned down at the beginning of the eighteenth century. The result of an act of carelessness on the part of a maid with her night candle. The new house, built with the help and input of Humphrey Repton, who had built other grand houses and landscaped other great parks in the area, had, in consequence, been one of the main centres for the English Landscape Movement he had been an important part of.

The Moorecroft family at that time were bankers, and therefore had plenty of other people's money to hand to spend on any work they wanted to carry out, like landscaping the garden, or renovating the house. They continued that way for the next century or two then, in the early nineteen hundreds, the last of the family, a spinster sister, faced with a huge bill for death duties on the death of her brother, who was killed fighting on the Western Front during the First World War, escaped paying them by presenting the house and estate to the nation. The nation hadn't really wanted either of them so had, instead, set up a trust fund to administer the house and grounds and open them to the public.

This arrangement had proved very successful. The farm lands were let to a succession of tenants, who provided income for the trust. The house and gardens were opened to the public for much of the year. The trust employed some staff to maintain the gardens, some to see to the running of the house, and others to see to its repair and upkeep. Between Easter and Michaelmas there was also a seasonal staff of tour guides – about twelve in all - who showed people around the house and gardens and around some of the farm areas if there were such things as lambing, or shoeing horses, or ploughing going on. Any form of farming activity the public would be prepared to pay to watch being done, in fact, whilst being very thankful they no longer had to do such things themselves.

A year or two before I had gone there to work there had been a new attraction introduced. A ghost walk. Someone on the management team had visited a similar garden in a different part of the country, which did have a ghost or two, and held a number of events there involving ghost walks around the most haunted parts of the grounds. This had seemed such a good idea to the people managing Moorecroft House when they found out about it, and had been told that the attraction brought a great deal of money into the coffers of the other garden, that a management decision was taken to promote Moorecroft House in the same way during the darker, mistier autumn and winter days, when there weren't flowering plants, or autumn colours in the garden to draw in the paying public. The fact that the other garden really did have a ghost or two which could be used in this way, and Moorecroft House didn't, was of no account when the scent of potential American dollars was in the air, and a Grey Lady, said to race along the path where I was working from time to time, soon became one of the garden's advertised attractions, even though, according to the staff who were employed on the estate, she had never been seen or heard by anyone working there yet, and I for one fervently hoped she never would. Or at least not during the next hour or two.

I had been taken on to be one of the staff who tended the gardens. A lad at the time, fresh out of school, I had been employed as temporary cover for a girl who had taken time off to have a baby and had been pleased as punch to get the job until people, Eddie Ponting, the foreman, in particular, had started telling me ghost stories.

Not that the idea of such things as ghosts existing were completely alien to me. I had been brought up by a grandfather who taught me to believe in ghosts through him trying to communicate with the spirit world by tapping on table tops and other surfaces in conversation, he said, with the departed, to see what response he got.

He had a knowledge of spiritualism which went beyond the norm, and an interest in the spirit world he passed on to me, that gave me an understanding and acceptance of its existence, even though I never indulged in it myself. I had a healthy distrust of Ouija boards, spirit writing and the like, which allowed me to accept that they worked, without wanting any personal involvement with them.

His was an unconventional outlook on life however you looked at it. I was never really sure what he was hoping to achieve by his actions, or even what response he got, if response he did get. Only that he seemed to believe in it himself. Tall, balding, bespectacled. If I close my eyes I can picture him even now. Though he died when I was still quite young, not quite into my teens in fact, leaving me to find my own way in life, his unusual behaviour was bound to leave its mark on an impressionable mind.

Especially in the night, when restless trees tapped on windows to be let in, and starlings jockeyed for more favourable sleeping positions beneath the eaves of the house we had lived in. In those early days immediately after he'd died, when Aunt Maggie, who lived with us both as well, had taken over full responsibility for my upbringing, even the rattle of raindrops could send me diving deep down beneath the bed clothes, in the fear that my grandfather might be trying to communicate with me.

That was only during those early years though. When I was hardly grown. Before age and its widening experiences began to make me start to adopt a degree of pride in having had such an eccentric forebear. One on whose account I eventually set off on a train of thought which was to lead me, not only to come to accept my grandfather's belief in the spirit world which surrounded ours, but to unconventional beliefs of my own.

Aunt Maggie had been his eldest daughter and had inherited many of his spiritual beliefs. She would trot off to see a medium, or to take part in a séance, handbag in hand, looking for all the world as if she was going to bingo, or a WI meeting, and come back full of tales of this or that spirit the medium had been in touch with, and talk about it all as if it was the most natural thing in the world to be doing – which in *her* world I suppose it was.

At first after my grandfather died, and she had sole charge of me, she used to try to get me to go to with her to see the mediums, or to a séance, but though I did at first, I soon gave up once I was old enough to say no. Instead I developed my own ideas of the spirit world, which I kept hidden from her, suspecting they would have seemed as outlandish to her as hers were to most other people.

In the end, my aunt and I moved so far apart in our psychic outlooks, that I decided it was time for us to be far apart physically as well, and, as soon as I had left school and was able, moved out of the family home and went northwards looking for work.

My aunt raised no objection to this. Even if she could have done. And I'm not so sure that she could, because she had never been my legal guardian. All she asked was that I kept in touch and let her know what I was doing from time to time. I think she knew as well as I did that we were completely incompatible as house mates.

So I moved north, finding work as a gardener. Tending roses, hoeing flower beds, cutting grass. My movements were so regular and reliable as I moved about the few small gardens for which I was responsible, it was rumoured there were actually people who set their watches by where I was, and what I was doing at the time. A mistake, unless on their dials were included the phases of the moon. The craft in which I had found employment had, after all, been the earliest religion of all.

The gardens of Elysium. Paradise. The abode of the soul. Sacred lily and hallowed lotus. The Delphic Oracle, whose divinations were the outcome of trances induced by the chewing of laurel leaves, and the far older Egyptian tradition of tree worship, from which it had derived. My grandfather, I'm sure, would have been proud of the depth of my knowledge of the subject, and would have encouraged it if he had still been alive.

That was why I had gone for the job I had seen advertised in Church Stretton, as temporary gardener at Moorecroft House, which I'd felt somehow drawn towards when I'd seen it advertised. Almost as if my grandfather had been trying to make contact with me in some way and send me in that direction. And that wouldn't have been as surprising as it seems, because I had been lodging for a few weeks now in a house in Church Stretton run by a lady who reminded me of my aunt in so many ways, I often wondered if she too paid regular visits to a medium, and could have met my grandfather at a séance there.

The house where I was lodging was close enough to my new place of work for me to be able to get there quite easily and I already felt as if I belonged there, even though it was only the first morning. I was prepared to be friendly to anyone, even to a man whose initial appearance had made me think he was a ghost, and bring back memories I wasn't altogether comfortable with. I put that first impression behind me, and held my hand out for him to shake. "I'm Peter." I introduced myself.

"Pleased to meet you Peter." He said with a grave smile, but without taking my hand. "Or is it Pete?"

"Most people call me Peter."

"Well I'm not most people Peter, so I'm going to call you Pete." He smiled and studied me with piercing eyes, his head tilted to one side. "I expect everyone's been filling you with all sorts of stories about the Grey Lady and other ghosts, haven't they?"

"Just a few," I admitted. "Well mostly Eddie Ponting, the foreman, I suppose."

"They usually do with new people. Well, don't believe them, that's all."

"It isn't true what they say about the Grey Lady?" I asked eagerly, seeking reassurance.

"Not a lot of it." His smile broadened.

"So there isn't a ghost then?" I relaxed, expecting him to put my mind at rest about a possibility I didn't want it dwelling on but, instead…

"I didn't say *that* did I?" He contradicted sharply. The smile dying.

"What do you mean?"

"I said what they've been telling you about *the Grey Lady* isn't true. I didn't say *no* ghost story is true. Ghosts are just… I don't know….just distant echoes of forgotten lives, someone called them once. It's intense human emotions over the years that cause things to happen. Things like ghosts appearing. And a place as old as this is, has had lots of chances for intense human emotions to make things like that happen, and happen and happen again, in a never ending cycle. I could tell you stories…" he paused.

"Yes," I prompted, leaning the cutters against the hedge and turning away from my work. Relaxed enough in his presence now not to think he might be intending to do me any sort of harm. Interested, despite myself, in beliefs which weren't a hundred miles away from my own. "Go on."

"No. I don't think I should." He shook his head. "You're just a boy. Too young to be thinking about ghosts. Too young to know what makes people tick. What makes people do the things they do because of love."

"Love?" I prompted again.

"Don't look so surprised." He frowned, "I know you're thinking I don't look much like it now. No!" As I was about to plead genuine innocence of that. At the age I was then, and never having been in love myself, I had no idea at all what made other people fall in or out of it. "There was a time, though," my companion went on, "when I still had the looks good enough to make a woman fall in love with me. A woman like Frances." He looked away into the distance.

"Frances?" I prompted a third time. Not really ready yet to pick up the cutters and turn back to the hedge again.

"One of the tour guides." He turned towards me again. "Or at least she used to be one of the tour guides for a while." He took the pipe out of his pocket again and tapped it on the fencepost next to him. "Are you sure you haven't got a light?"

"Sorry, no." I emptied my pockets to prove it. "So she isn't anymore then?"

"What?" He looked back at me blankly.

"Frances," I prompted, putting back the things I had taken out of my pockets, "a tour guide?"

"No."

"But she was when you first came here?" I prompted again, as he continued to look back at me uncomprehendingly.

"No." He shook his head as if to clear it of something, some other thought which was getting in the way of the one he was trying to concentrate on. "There *was* a girl, then, when I first started, but it wasn't her. A fat, jolly girl whose name was….. what….I don't know…..I can't remember. Not memorable enough you see."

"Not like Frances?" I said brightly.

"Who?" He looked at me blankly again, obviously not welcoming my interrupting his thought processes like that.

"Frances." I prompted again, but he had lapsed into silence and I let him be. Finding the effort of talking to him harder work than the hedge cutting had been, I picked up the cutter, turned back to the hedge and got on with it. Expecting him to go off about his own business, whatever that was, but I was wrong, he wasn't done with me yet.

"I was one of the first, you know."

"One of the first?" I turned the hedge cutters off and, looking round reluctantly to where he stood staring at me again, put them down with a barely supressed sigh.

"Tour guides." My companion explained with a smile. "One of the first tour guides. I got talked into it by my friend, Phil, who had just signed on for his first season, himself, and got in touch with me when he decided it was a job which would suit me too, because of the hours and the chance to score with the women we were showing around if we fancied them.

Phil was really into that sort of thing, but I wasn't, not as much as him anyway. Oh I liked the girls as much as he did, but he was the love 'em and leave 'em type, whilst I was much more serious where girls were concerned. Believed there was only ever going to be one love in my life, who I would recognise and fall for at first sight, and who would be my soul mate for life after that. And that was what happened. Unfortunately." He blinked and wiped at his eye as if he'd suddenly got a bit of dust in it.

"Unfortunately?" I repeated, blinking a little myself at ideas that weren't a million miles away from my own.

"Yes."

"Why unfortunately?" I probed.

"Because what I hadn't planned for, or expected, was for the girl I fell in love with to be married." He stood, apparently lost in thought at the memory of it, and when he didn't come back from wherever it was memory had taken him, I picked up the cutters and turned back to the hedge again, determined not to let myself be interrupted by him anymore, and risk getting into my new employers bad books by not doing my work properly.

CHAPTER TWO

"Have you ever thought of studying for a degree?" The little man in Elizabethan clothing asked suddenly, speaking almost into my ear, so I could hear him above the noise of the machinery I was wielding.

"What?" He'd been sunk in silence so long I'd forgotten his continued presence there. Now I stepped back a pace or two from the hedge and turned round again, hedge cutters still going. Startled by the sudden change of direction.

"A degree. It's why a lot of us tour guides take the job. It's seasonal work, and has funny hours, but it gives us time to study as well. Especially on days when it's raining, and nobody much comes in wanting to be shown around the place." He was almost shouting now so I could hear him above the sound of the cutters, and couldn't easily ignore him.

"I'm not a tour guide, remember." I reminded him sharply. "I'm a gardener."

"Oh yes. Of course! I forgot."

"Are you studying for one then? A degree?"

"Yes." He replied with a self-satisfied smirk on his face.

"What in?" I thought I'd better ask, even if I wasn't really that interested.

"What do you think?" He asked. Still with that same smirk on his face.

"I don't know." I'd thought he'd given up on me, and was leaving me to get on with my work in peace, so when I now found that he hadn't, I answered a little irritably. "I don't know what they do them in." I turned the hedge cutters off again.

"Most of the subjects you studied at school I expect, and a few more besides." He answered into the silence. "So what do you think I might be studying?"

"I really don't know." I said more irritably still.

"Guess." He persisted. Ignoring my obvious reluctance to join in his private 'Twenty Questions' session.

"History." I plucked a subject out of the ether at random. Just to shut him up really.

"History!" He snorted dismissively. "Why would I study that? What use would it be to *me*?"

"A lot of use in a place like this I would have thought." And I would have, when I'd had time to reflect on what my reply had been.

"Then you'd have thought wrong. I'm studying with the Royal Academy of Music, or hoping to, when I've got enough money together to pay for a course, and then find a way of carrying on my studying whilst I'm still working here if they'll let me. I'm hoping to study for a degree in performance art and composition, with the lute as my main instrument." He smiled at me complacently. "Learning how to write songs to go with it eventually, I hope."

"The lute!" I exclaimed.

"Yes, the lute. Why not?" he said, his smile vanishing, obviously irritated by my lack of support. "You sound a bit surprised."

"Not really a lot of call for people to be playing lutes these days I'd have thought," I said judgementally, leaning on my cutters.

"I suppose *you* think I ought to be playing a guitar like all the others do?" He frowned.

"Yes," I nodded. "That, or a moog synthesiser, anyway."

"A *what*?" He glared. Apparently annoyed at my presumption in disagreeing with him.

"Moog synthesiser." I repeated defensively. Not really sure I'd got the word right.

"Don't know what that is I'm afraid."

"An electronic synthesiser that reproduces the sounds of different musical instruments, so you can sound as if you've got a whole orchestra behind you, instead of just the one keyboard playing. Invented by a Dr Robert Moog. I think Elton John plays one sometimes as a change from playing the piano." Hoping to impress him, I aired my complete knowledge of the subject. Information about it I'd forgotten I was in possession of.

He remained resolutely unimpressed. "Elton *Who*?" He looked me up and down like something he would have liked to have stepped on.

"John. Elton John. You must have heard of *him. He* studied with the Royal Academy of Music too." I pulled out another little gem of information I'd completely forgotten I was in possession of until that moment.

"Afraid not." He continued unimpressed, "Can't be one of their more successful students, or I would have heard of him." I decided not to argue, but just cut my losses and move the conversation on by asking.

"Why a lute?"

"Don't know really," he replied after a moment or two's consideration. "Just an instrument I've always felt drawn to learning to play for some reason."

"Didn't they use to play them in the olden days?" I was off showing off my little bit of knowledge again. "Pre Beatles."

"Pre *what*?" He looked back at me blankly.

"Not what." I corrected him. "Who. Pre who. The Beatles."

"You've lost me again I'm afraid." He shook his head, brow wrinkled in thought.

I looked at him in exasperation, but decided to let it pass. If he wanted to pretend he was too highbrow in his musical tastes to have heard of any contemporary musicians I supposed that was his business. "Never mind," I said, "tell me about the lute. Isn't it a thing like a ukulele with a bent handle they used to play in Elizabethan times?"

He blanched a little at my description of his chosen instrument, drew in a sharp breath as if about the challenge it, then seemed to decide the chance of airing some of his own knowledge was too good to miss, so did that instead. "Yes, that was their heyday," he agreed, "but people probably started playing them in England in the twelve hundreds and from then on every court in the land had a lute player or two right down through the middle ages.

In the late fourteen hundreds lutes became an emblem of the renaissance, and very popular amongst the nobility. Manuscripts of lute music began to appear around 1500 and court poets like Thomas Wyatt sang their poetry to music played on the lute.

Somebody, and I don't remember who, but it was bound to have been a French lord of some sort, once said that to an Englishman an intellectual is someone who thinks up clever ways of seducing other men's wives. One of which ways was either by getting a troubadour to serenade her on their behalf with his lute, or by doing it themselves. Most English lute players eventually gave up playing the more classical forms of the music, such as love songs, in favour of playing pavans, galliards and almans, which were all forms of folk music really." He smiled knowingly. "I preferred writing and playing the love songs though."

"I thought you hadn't learned to play them yet." I cut in on his reminiscences. If he was going to bore me with them, he might at least try to keep track of them himself.

"What?" He looked back at me blankly. His train of thought apparently gone.

"The lute." I said sternly. "Or the love songs. I thought you hadn't learned to play either of them yet."

He shook his head as if to clear it of something. Looking at me as if he was trying to remember something. To draw back a thought which wouldn't quite come for some reason. "I've always been able to *that*," he contradicted. "To win a girl's heart with my music and my songs. I'm hoping to write a musical one day," He said triumphantly, as if he had scored a point off me in some strange sort of private game he was playing with me.

"Are you?" I picked up the cutters in my hand and turned back to the hedge again, my mind made up this time. I was going to get on with my work and not allow him to interrupt me anymore. "If you say so."

"You aren't much fun you know," he said critically, as I turned away. "Just like Phil in a lot of ways."

"Phil?" My finger hovered over the starter button, but I didn't press it. He'd caught my attention just in time, damn him, and I let him take me back into a past I was destined to spend a lot of time in that day.............
....
........"My friend Phil." He smiled at the memory. Oblivious to my presence again I was sure. "The one I told you about who talked me into becoming a tour guide with him. You know," he shook his head in apparent disbelief, "he didn't believe I could foresee the future. Even when I told him over a drink in the pub one night that something was coming, that I could feel it in my water."

"Something?" Phil prompted in response, studying me across the top of an empty beer glass he was waiting for me to get refilled for him. "What?"

"I don't know, Phil," I answered fretfully. "It's just that…well, you know the tingling I get in my fingertips when something good is about to happen to me?"

"The tingling you *say* you get in your fingertips when something good is about to happen to you," he tapped the bottom of the glass impatiently on the table.

"I've got it all over me!" I ended triumphantly.

"Hmmm." His eyes flicked briefly and almost imperceptibly towards heaven. "With anyone else I'd say they'd probably been mixing with the wrong kind of woman, but as it's you.... Heat rash perhaps?"

"It isn't that hot at the moment." I contradicted, irritated by his attitude, despite it being no more than I would have expected of him.

"Well maybe it's going to be. I don't know. What do *you* think is causing it?"

"I told you. Something's coming."

"Yes, but *what*?"

I shrugged. "It's Imbolc next week. Maybe *that's* got something to do with it."

"Imbolc?" He repeated slowly. Raising his eyes heavenwards.

"When the Goddess returns from the Otherworld and the Earth rejoices. Candlemas in the Christian calendar. A time of change and new beginnings after the passing of winter. I'm surprised you didn't know that. I thought you knew everything."

"I know that it's about time you got your round in." he interrupted, stung into the abandonment of tact and diplomacy by my gentle dig at his reputation as a fount of all knowledge. "Coming of the Goddess after winter! What possible credence can outlandish ideas like those have in the modern world? You spend far too much time thinking about that sort of thing!".........

....

......Geoff Truscott broke off the story he was telling and looked at me keenly. "I suppose *you* think those are pretty outlandish ideas as well, don't you?" He asked perceptively. "Just like Phil did."

"Well I…." I got no further before he interrupted.

"I can see it in your face, so you needn't pretend. Most people would agree with you too, I'm sure. I suppose I never really grew up in that respect, though. Always preferring stories with happy endings rather than reality. Always preferring love stories to kitchen sink dramas. I suppose that was why I let Frances enchant me the way she did."

"Enchant you?"

"Well there must have been an *element* of enchantment in it mustn't there?" He said thoughtfully. "Why else would I have behaved so out of character whenever she was around? To fall in love with her at first sight like that. I mean, I didn't do that sort of thing. Not at first sight. Not at all until I met *her*. That was why other people…. Well, I mean….and going after a married woman. That *too*. Not *my* style at all. That was why people who'd known me before I met her found it so hard to handle. They all thought I'd come to my senses once the initial attraction had passed, but I never did." He shook his head again, as if still trying to clear his thoughts, and smiled sadly. "I'm getting a bit ahead of myself here telling you about Frances, who was still in the future when I was having that drink with Phil. One of the last I ever had with him before our relationship changed forever."

"Why?"

"Do you mean why was it one of our last drinks together, or why did our relationship change forever?"

"Either. Both. I don't know." I retreated quickly from giving a direct answer to the sudden questioning.

"Nor did I, then. Just knew something was coming, and told Phil, who was very disbelieving about it."

"Oh yeah?" He said, scathingly. "Well if it does, I'll buy every round for the next six months!"

It was an offer I ought really to have taken him up on, because my mother's old dog died the following

evening, and his death seemed to be the firsts of a sequence of events which would see my way of life change forever...
....

CHAPTER THREE

......"Do you know Ian Wallace?" Geoff Truscott, who I had decided by now probably *wasn't* a ghost, asked suddenly. Staring at me with a frown, as he broke into his own story again.

"Ian Wallace"? I don't think so." I replied, shaking my head, taken off guard. "Who is he? Another friend of yours?"

"An old time singer. Before your time probably. And not to your taste either. No moog synthesiser you see." He smiled and turned his head sideways, looking at me birdlike. "That *was* what you called it, wasn't it?"

"It *was*." I answered, surprised but strangely gratified that he'd remembered. I'd noticed older people didn't always remember things I told them. Didn't consider them important enough, probably.

"Well, he used to sing a song about a farmer leaning on a gate staring at the spot where his lurcher is buried. A really sad song, guaranteed to bring tears to anybody's eyes. And that just about summed up *my* feelings after I'd backfilled the grave I'd dug for the dog under an apple tree at the bottom end of the garden the next day. I've got the record in my collection somewhere.

Not that my mother's dog was a lurcher – whatever they are." He went off at an apparent tangent again. "I've never been sure."

"Cross between a greyhound and a collie aren't they?" I answered. Getting used to his habit of breaking into his own stories and taking the chance again to air the little knowledge I had on a subject.

"Might be. I don't know." He paused, collecting his thoughts. "How did we get on to that anyway?"

"Your mother's dog dying."

"Oh yeah." He stopped to gather his thoughts for a moment before going on..."I'd still been living at home when my mother bought the dog. Too soon after a previous dog on which she'd doted had died, I thought. She hadn't always been as loving towards him as she ought to have been because of that, so I'd tried to compensate for the rough deal I thought he was getting from her.

A mistake that. There's nothing quite like a pair of soulful brown eyes gazing up adoringly into yours for dragging out a man's protective instincts the way that dog had dragged out mine.

I'd been away from the family home for quite a few years by then, by the time I'm talking about when the dog died, I mean, sharing my life with Caroline, a widow woman who had a house of her own too. For a while we were so close and spent so much time in each other's company and each other's houses, we were practically living together, but she wasn't content with that, and wanted to make our relationship 'respectable' as she called it, by marrying me. Something I wasn't prepared to do until I'd met the right woman, and I knew that wasn't Caroline, so in the end we went our separate and respectable ways. I don't think Caroline ever really forgave me for it though, and was usually very frosty with me on the odd occasion that we bumped into each other after that.

I'd been completely on my own for a year or so since Caroline's ultimatum to me about making ourselves respectable, or splitting up, at the time I'm talking about, and I used to go back to my parent's house most weekends – my father was still alive then – to have lunch with them, and to play with the dog. When I came out into the hall that evening after I'd been back there for Sunday dinner, and saw the old dog lying there with his eyes still glazing over in what seemed to have been the most peaceful of deaths, it was as if his passing somehow signified the ending of an era for me.

I said as much to Phil, but he wasn't at all sympathetic."

"It was only a dog." He answered. "Buy your mother another."

"I don't know that she wants another dog." I said. "They don't have long enough lives for one thing, and there's too much pain involved in losing them. I've invited her to come and live with me for a few weeks until she gets over it. She's all on her own now. And it's almost the first anniversary of my dad dying too."

"A mistake Geoff. Once she's got a foothold in your house she won't want to leave again." Phil always saw himself as an authority on how I should live my life and was always too ready to be laying down the law about it I thought. We had known each other so long now, I often felt that it was only the years which held us together. Shared boyhood memories turning us into the platonic equivalent of those long married couples who know each other's weaknesses so well that it's purely out of habit, rather than for any actual reason, when they exploit them.

"I don't think so, Phil." I contradicted him sharply. "What does it matter anyway? There's nothing much in my life at the moment she could *try* to interfere with is there? Not since I stopped being with Caroline." I blithely ignored all the portents I'd been telling him about only the week before.

"Then you've both got what you want, so why worry about it?" He changed to what was a more interesting topic of conversation for him. Women. "Did you notice who Hargreaves was showing around the other morning? Our new workmate. A seasonal tour guide. Taking the place of Belinda, he said. Gone off to travel around the world with some friends Belinda has, so won't be joining us this year. Now *she* looked worth a little of *anyone's* time."

I studied my companion uneasily. Middle thirties, and not only very good looking, but with an ego and a depth of knowledge of his subject which made him the star tour guide at Moorecroft House, and its acknowledged stud as well. Phil's silvery-tongued ways had stood him in good stead as long as I had known him. Not just when showing visitors around the house either. He seemed quite able, given enough time, to talk any woman into bed with him.

"Did he introduce you to her?" Even as I looked at him, Phil's pupils were dilating quite alarmingly.

"After a fashion I suppose," he replied. "You know Hargreaves though. So soft spoken I could hardly make out what he said. Her name is Frances Delamore though."

"Frances Delamore?" I repeated carefully. Trying the name out for size. "She's not English then?"

"Yes, she is." He contradicted. "Got a French husband though."

"Hargreaves told you all that?" I showed my surprise.

"No." Eyes narrower now, Phil was obviously reliving the moment. "He didn't need to," he smiled. "I figured most of it out myself. She was wearing a ring, but I would have known she was married in any case. There's a certain look about married women. Something you get to recognise if you study them enough."

"Does it make you tingle?" I wanted to ask him, but decided instead to stay dumb. I've got another song somewhere in my record collection about love coming with rockets, stars and poetry. When Frances Delamore, a woman of about the same age as me, had been brought into the rest room and introduced to us all I had been embarrassed by a voice in my head which screamed so suddenly loudly that I was convinced it must be audible to everyone around. "This is it! This is her! The something you've been so long waiting for! The coming of the Goddess, and the changing of the pattern of your life!"

I finished my drink with Phil, taking care not to make any further reference to Frances which might stimulate any interest in her on his part. He was quite heavily committed at the time, even by his standards, and I relied on that to keep him from any immediate attempt to add her to his tally, whilst I tried to make up my mind exactly what I ought to do.

I had been working at Moorecroft House for no more than a few months myself at the time, and rather liked the place. It was my fellow tour guides I sometimes found difficult to stomach, intent as they were on talking shop all the while. Even during rest periods when I would have much preferred to be reading something related to my studies. Unwilling to add my own bass to the hubbub of voices, amidst which not one person was even pretending to listen to anyone else, I had tried at first to retreat behind the upraised pages of a book on occasions, but interruptions were frequent, and it had proved difficult to concentrate. Worse, I was only too well aware that in the eyes of my fellow members of staff my behaviour, though arguably better mannered than theirs, simply did not conform.

Phil hadn't told me it would be like that when he'd talked me into applying for the job there and then put in the word or two which ensured that I got it. I wanted desperately to fit in, but was finding it hard going. Now the vision of loveliness in brown laced up dress and bright red under bodice, with green pinafore pinned to the front of it – the female tour guides costume for the day - who had had such an effect on me, offered a friendly face amongst so many disgruntled, or disinterested ones, but she presented a worrying distraction for me too, as I found myself day dreaming about undoing the laced up front of her dress to discover what lay beneath.

Two cardinal rules of my life had always been not to get emotionally involved with anyone I worked with, and never, ever, to set my cap at a married woman.

"Don't allow yourself into any situation where you can become involved," I had once told Phil when he had protested that it was not always avoidable, "and it has no way of happening. You have to strike a match to get the spark to start a fire."

"And what about those spontaneous fires of heath or grassland they sometimes get on the Long Mynd, when the heat alone is enough to cause combustion?" he could have replied if he'd been interested enough to argue. And after meeting Frances I would have found it difficult, if not impossible, to counter that attack.

Not that I didn't try to hold back from what in my heart of hearts I knew was inevitable, now the woman my soul itself recognised to be its mate in life, had come so close.

I avoided Frances as much as was humanly possible. I ignored her presence completely whenever she drew too near. Brought a solitary side of my nature, I hadn't known I had before, to such a fine pitch that no one could possibly have known how to do so was tearing the guts out of me. My temper may have been a little bit sharper than usual, my tolerance level lower than before, but, not knowing what I was like under normal circumstances, the difference in my behaviour when she was around probably wasn't apparent to Frances. If she thought of me at all, I doubt if it was other than to consider me a very unfriendly person.

It couldn't go on of course. *That* state of affairs. Hiding your feelings about someone depends on either being able to avoid them altogether, or else having so many other people about, that their attention can be distracted, or distorted, in some way. Though the numbers of the regular staff of tour guides were boosted by extra seasonal staff during the summer months to cover such contingencies as staff holidays, sickness amongst the seasonal staff, coupled with the actual staff vacations they were supposed to be providing cover for, robbed me of the cover which the other members of staff had been providing. Even Hargreaves would be out of the country for a week or two. A fortnight during which, apart from the maintenance staff out and about in the gardens and the administrative staff tucked away in their ground floor offices, there would only be the two of us around, unless the ones on sick leave returned quickly. And they didn't.

Even so, I still tried to fight on a little by not going to the rest room for tea. Just slipping in and out of the offices to collect the daily rota when I felt it was safe to do so. Going into the men's changing rooms to put on my costume and then slipping out of the back door to collect the visitors I was going to be taking around and showing the attractions of the place. All the while avoiding the person who, for me at least, offered the greatest attraction of all - Frances. All right until she sought me out to ask me why I was being so elusive lately. How could I possibly explain that it was simply a last desperate effort on my part to hold back from telling her I was in love with her.

So we drank our tea and we ate our biscuits together, and she told me about her husband, Jean, who she had met whilst she was living in France some years before. Just after the war. He was the son of a hotelier, with five hotels in a ski resort at the edge of the Alps, and had been so in love with her that he had followed her to England when she'd returned home.

Taking my turn after that, I found myself talking to her as I had never ever talked to *anyone* before. My hopes, my schemes, my music and my life so far. Even about sharing my life with Caroline, and how we'd been unable to make a go of things. I laid it all before her as naturally as if I had been discussing such intimate matters with comparative strangers all my life.

It took just three days to arrive at a point where I told Frances of my feelings for her. Not directly, because I wasn't experienced enough in the course on which I was embarking, that of declaring my love to *anyone*, never mind a married woman, to commit myself too easily and risk being put down by her for my complete misreading of the situation.

In the end it was by way of the words of a lyric I'd been working on for some weeks that I decided to make my longings known to her.

It was one I had actually composed about Frances when I had first seen her, and had then set to music as part of my presentation for entrance to the Royal Academy of Music. To sing it to her would have required me bringing my lute along to accompany myself on, and I decided that would be too difficult to manage, so I thrust a copy of it into her hand as she was going home, hoping that reading the sentiment expressed in it would tell her more clearly what my feelings for her were than anything I might try to say.

"Is it funny?" She asked awkwardly, as she took it from me, and I breathed a silent, but fervent, prayer that she wouldn't find it so.

I arrived at work for my afternoon session the next day to find Frances waiting me in the car park. "I'm confused," she confessed. "No one has ever written something like that about me before."

It seemed the perfect cue for me to whisk her off into the cover of the woodland which bounded the car park, take her into my arms and confuse her even more.

Diffidently at first, because, despite what her immediate response had been, I still half expected my actions to lead to a scathing rejection in the end, but with increasing passion as her parted lips signalled willingness and more, and my pent up feelings were given free rein at last.

"No!" she gasped finally, pushing me away from her. "No! This can't be happening to me. I love my husband. I'm a happily married woman!"

But it *had* happened, and it *was* happening, and would continue to do so as Frances fought as hard to forestall any further advances on my part as I had previously fought to prevent myself from getting to the point where there was no way of avoiding their being made.

There were times when just looking at her caused me actual physical pain, so deep was my need for her. There were times when I was so twisted up by worries about what I had set in motion, I was unable to sleep.

I had long since given up eating any of the sandwiches I brought into work with me each day and only picked at my evening meal. My usually healthy appetite had vanished overnight. Pale and wan, I would hurry into work each day impatient for the first of the tea breaks and the dinner break when Frances and I would be together, extending them for as long as we dared. Cold cups of liquid tipped away at the end of each break spoke volumes of how little interest in their true purpose we had and all the while the precious days of our solitude hurried past us at an alarming rate.

So came all too soon the day which was to be our last spent with just each other for company. Frances was going to France with her husband to visit his family the following week, and by the time she came back, even if the sick ones amongst the tour guides hadn't returned to work, the ones who were on holiday definitely would have done. And after that there would only be a few months before her term as seasonal tour guide was over. In the frame of mind of prisoners knowing there is to be no stay of execution, but intent on enjoying what little time still remains, we took the afternoon off and went for a walk together down by the river in Ludlow.

It was warm and sunny and under different circumstances it could have been paradise to lose ourselves amidst the anonymity of the crowds there. As it was though, the reality of imminent parting brooded over us like a dark cloud, and our hands gripped each other's tightly, as if to postpone the evil moment when we finally had to let go.

"My god you're beautiful!" I'd stopped and held her at arms length for a moment to study her face in detail, careless of how avoiding action on the part of other walkers was necessitated by the sudden appearance of an obstacle in their path.

"I know," she answered flippantly, turning away from a scrutiny she obviously found too close for comfort.

"And I'm in love with you."

"I know that too," she pulled me out of the way of a two seater pushchair, which was being sturdily propelled past us, regardless of any minor impediment such as that represented by my legs. Its single occupant, thumb in mouth, looked back at us with interest as it hurried on. "At least I know that you like to think that you are. We're causing an obstruction here. Shall we move on?"

"*Think* I am!" I took her hand again as I did as I was bid. "I *know* I am!"

"With the idea perhaps. Ask yourself though. How can you be in love with me after - what is it now - *eight days*? I think you use the word too easily."

"One hundred and ninety eight hours, ten minutes and fifteen seconds if you mean since I first kissed you. Six months though, since I set eyes on you that morning and loved you at first sight."

"Hmm. So you keep telling me."

"And so you keep refusing to believe. Or refusing to admit that you believe. I'm never really quite sure which."

"Oh the first one I'm afraid. I'm simply not into inspiring such grand passion at first sight. It isn't me. Nor is this hole in the wall, sneaking down back alleys, business. I'm trading on years of trust which hasn't been misplaced until now," she said with a trace of bitterness in her voice. "I looked at Jean last night and wondered - *Why*? Why is this happening to me? I still love him as much as ever. It's just that I somehow love you more and in a different way from the way I love him. I suppose it's because there's no passion between us anymore. We've been together so long that we were just sort of comfortable in each other's ways. Now *you've* come along and there's a barrier growing up between us. I don't know if I can ever forgive you for that." She glared at me so fiercely I took her hand more firmly for fear she was going to turn away from me there and then, and we pushed our way further into the crowd and into a future together.

That was the first time we ever walked anywhere where we could enjoy the anonymity of being lost in

amongst a crowd of people like that. And it was to be a while before we went back to the river again. Usually when we wanted to be spontaneously alone for some reason. Away from the prying eyes of our fellow tour guides. We would walk along by the serpentine canal at the far end of the grounds of Moorecroft House. That was where we used to go to talk things through in the early days of us being together, if for some reason we couldn't actually manage to get off site. Far enough away from the centre of things for us not to be noticed by our fellow workers we hoped. A place which become an anathema to me eventually, because it was always there where we went to thrash out any problems which occurred in our relationship.................................
....
......Have you ever been there?" Geoff suddenly asked, breaking into his account to do so.

"I don't think so." So engrossed in his story was I by then, that it took me a moment or two to register that he was directing a question at me.

"Not really had time to go anywhere yet I suppose. I keep forgetting that this is only your first morning here. And is that the clock I can hear striking the hour? What time is it?"

I consulted my watch. "Twelve o'clock."

"Your lunchtime. You'd better get off, or they'll be sending out a search party for you. You going to be back here this afternoon?"

"Probably. Depends on Eddie Ponting, the foreman, I suppose."

"Don't tell him you've been wasting your time talking to me – all right, *listening* to me. If you *are* here after lunch I might tell you the next bit of my story. Now that's an incentive for anyone!" He laughed. "See you then."

"See you." I picked up my tools, put them all in the barrow, and made my way slowly back to the bothy.

CHAPTER FOUR

"You don't seem to have got much work done young Peter. I've been following you around and I have to say I couldn't really see where you'd been." Eddie Ponting, large and balding, and still wearing a T shirt advertising the Isle of Wight festival of 1970, when half a million teenagers swamped the island to attend the first ever outdoor pop festival starring Joan Baez, The Rolling Stones and the Who, to name just a few, probably the only act of rebellion in his otherwise law abiding life, studied me over the top of his glasses, as he looked up from his newspaper when I sat down opposite him at the table in the bothy and reached into my bag for the packet of sandwiches I'd brought to work with me.

"You've been checking up on me?" I answered sharply, feeling guilty about how little work I'd done that morning.

"Don't get saucy now." He frowned irritably, "It's what I'm paid to do."

"Yes, sorry, I guess it is." I was immediately contrite. After all, it was my first morning there. "Well, if I don't seem to have got much done you'll have to blame Geoff. He kept talking at me all morning."

"Geoff?" I could see he really wanted to get back to his newspaper and read about what the England cricket team had been getting up to the previous day, but was too aware of the responsibilities of his position as foreman to do that now.

"Geoff Truscott. He said he was one of the tour guides."

"Tour guides? They don't normally bother themselves with the likes of us. What did you say his name was?"

"Geoff Truscott."

"Can't say I know him. Do you Joe?" He directed the question at a tall, thin, man sitting in one of the armchairs by the fireplace.

Joe looked up from his newspaper, equally reluctantly, and seemed to consider the question before replying. "No. Must be one of the new ones. They're always changing." He looked back down at his newspaper as if daring either of us to interrupt his reading again.

"He said he'd been working here almost since the place opened." I contradicted him uneasily. Reluctant to give offence.

"We ought to know him then." Eddie commented.

"But you don't." I took a bite of the sandwich I'd been unwrapping as he spoke. Cheese and pickle.

"No. What was he like?"

"I don't know." I spoke through a mouthful of food. "Small and dark. Dressed in Elizabethan clothes."

"Dressed in Elizabethan clothes?" Eddie sounded surprised at that.

"Yes." I took a swig of the mug of tea I'd poured for myself from the pot on the stove.

"Why?" He asked, giving me an old fashioned look.

"Because he was a tour guide." I answered simply.

"Why would he be dressed as an Elizabethan because he was a tour guide?" Joe looked up from his newspaper again, sounding a little bemused.

"He said it was their costume." I explained.

"Tour guides don't normally wear costumes." Eddie said sharply. Looking as if he thought I might be making the whole thing up.

"Oh."

"Look here Peter," he went on, glaring over his spectacles at me, "are you having a joke with us to pay us back for telling you to look out for the Grey Lady?"

"A joke to pay you back?" I hoped I sounded as upset by that idea as he obviously was. "On my first morning here! I just wanted to get my head down and do a good job so you kept me on. I was grateful for the work."

His frown faded, and I began to breathe a little more easily again. "Okay Peter. You might not have been playing a trick on *us*, but it seems to me as if someone might have been playing one on *you*. Tell you what I'm going to do. I'm going to come along with you when you go back after this break and see the bloke for meself."

"See I'm not making it all up, you mean?"

"Well it does seem a funny story. I'd take you to see Montgomery, the senior tour guide, but he isn't in today, so we'll have to sort it out ourselves." He was on his feet, putting newspaper and empty sandwich bag back in his knapsack, and rinsed out mug upside down on the draining board, by then. "Come on."

"What?" I had just got myself settled into the spare seat in the bothy, and my own newspaper spread out on the table in front of me.

"It's one o'clock. Time to get back to work. You were late coming in, remember?" He headed out of the door.

I swallowed a quick mouthful of tea, shoved the last piece of cheese and pickle into my mouth, the newspaper back into my bag, and followed him as he hurried out of the yard and down the path towards the haunted track. Hurrying ahead of me, but wasting his time, as I had been half afraid he would be, because of my friend of the morning there was no sign, even though Eddie hung about for as long as he could, before having to give up and go off about his own work, promising to come back again to check up on me before the afternoon break.

I watched him go, and then got on with the hedge cutting, or would have done if that now familiar voice hadn't spoken from behind the fringe of bushes which bordered the other side of the path.

"Has he gone?"

"You know full well he has." I said accusingly, putting the hedge cutters down again. "You waited until then before you made yourself known."

"Now why would I do that?" He smiled easily.

"Because you're not really a tour guide." I accused.

"Is that what he told you?" His smile widened.

"Yes."

"What am I then? A ghost?"

"You might well be for all I know. Certainly someone with a very strange sense of humour."

"An expensive one too, if it runs to kitting myself out like this just to play a prank on you." He commented, indicating his clothes by the movement of his hands.

I looked at him, blinked, and then looked again. He was no longer dressed in Elizabethan doublet and hose, but in the tall hat with broad brim, short straight jacket, long cloak, short trousers, and wide-topped boots of the puritan era, usually associated with the pilgrim fathers, and was carrying, not a corn cob pipe, but a long stemmed clay pipe. Still unlit.

"Look!" I stormed, stepping forward a few paces so I could look him directly in the eyes. "I don't *care* who or what you are! It's my first day of working here and all I wanted to do was make a good impression on the people I work with, so it isn't my *last* day too. So will you please leave me alone, so I can get on with my hedge cutting!"

"So you don't want to hear the rest of my story?"

"Frankly no. I'm not interested in you, or your story. I just want to get on with my work, Geoff!"

"Geoff." He looked me up and down with an unfathomable expression on his face. "Why did you call me Geoff?"

"Because it's your name." I answered simply.

"No it's not." He contradicted flatly.

"It's what you said your name was when you introduced yourself to me this morning. Geoff Truscott." I said coldly. Studying him more closely. Less certain now. "It *was* you who spoke to me this morning wasn't it? Even though you're dressed differently now."

"My name is Walter Moraine." He returned my stare steadily.

"Walter Moraine." I repeated, feeling sure I was in a bad dream I hoped I'd wake up from very soon.

He laughed. "You should see your face! It's a picture. You don't know *what* to believe do you?"

I swallowed hard. "So you are Geoff Truscott then?"

"Of course."

"Why are you dressed differently though?"

"I told you I have to change my costume to suit what it is I'm showing people, didn't I?"

I looked around us very pointedly, before turning back to glare at him. "*What* people? There aren't any. And why did Eddie and Joe say they'd never heard of you? *Or* tour guides dressing up in costumes either?"

He pulled a face. "Perhaps I'd better tell you the rest of my story. Then you might begin to understand."

"I don't think I *want* to hear it, or to *understand* it." I stepped back a little way away from him. "I just want to get on with my work. Now, I can't stop you talking to me if you're intent on doing that, but I certainly don't have to listen to you if I don't want to. You'll just be wasting your time if you go on, but feel free to do so if you want to." I turned my back on him, started the cutters, revved them a few times, then deliberately let the noise of them drown out whatever he was trying to say.

CHAPTER FIVE

"If you don't listen to me you'll never know whether I'm a ghost or not." My companion came up close to me and spoke directly into my ear. So I couldn't go on ignoring him.

"I don't want to know." I answered firmly. Turning the cutters off none the less, because, whatever I pretended to the irritating little man, he had caught my attention with his story, and I *did* want to hear more of it.

"Really?" He said disbelievingly.

"Really." I answered as positively as I could manage to appear under the circumstances.

"But what have you got to lose if you do?" He asked artlessly.

"My job, if I don't get any more work done than I did this morning." I replied. "Eddie Ponting was more understanding than he might have been under the circumstances. He could have made much more of a fuss. I think he was more annoyed at *you* than he was at me as it turned out."

"People in this place often are." He frowned. "Always have been where I'm concerned. Don't like people who don't toe the line."

"Like you, you mean?" I switched the cutters on again and turned purposefully back towards the hedge, revving them loudly to emphasise my intentions.

"Yes." He said, glaring at me defiantly, as if I was likely to agree with that assessment of his shortcomings.

"You can't blame them if you're always carrying on like you have done today." I commented critically.

"They wouldn't have minded if that was all I'd done *then*." He said ruminatively, his mind going back to the events again. "It was me falling in love with Frances they couldn't handle when they found out about it."

"They *did* find out about it then?" I was interested despite myself. Switching the cutters off as I turned to face him again.

"Couldn't hope to hide it from them really, could we? Not being so close to each other, and amongst such a small group of people. Even then, they could have simply ignored it and given us chance to burn ourselves out if they'd wanted to, but they didn't, and probably made the whole thing more intense by their attitude towards us. Even Phil, who shouldn't have had the gall to interfere at all, with *his* record with women, had to get himself involved. In fact he was the first to bring out into the open what the others were saying about us............
....
......."A word to the wise." He said to me one Monday morning, a month or so after Frances had returned from her visit to France, not wanting to tell me anything about it, but having apparently missed me as much as I had been missing her whilst we were apart.

Stopping to speak to me as he was passing on his way to take one of his early session tour groups, Phil had said languidly, "You mightn't be aware of it Geoff, but your peccadillo has become a subject for full and frank discussion in the rest room of late."

"Has it?" I wasn't really interested. Only surprised it had taken so long for anyone to notice what was going on between us, when every break spent there was a hell of inconsequential chatter in a room full of potential witnesses to the way in which every look which passed between the two of us must have cried out aloud our feelings for each other. Only amongst people as wrapped up in themselves as tour guides are could our blatant body language have passed so unremarked until now.

"They're even saying that you've been seen down the back lane to Acton Hall together at dinnertime and you know what everyone is going to make of that?"

Only too well, I thought to myself as he spoke, but then people will make anything what they choose to make it anyway. To me the narrow, pot-holed lane, where the local riding stables hid its rougher hacks on stunted scrub and sparse stands of grass, was where I had driven with Frances during that first week of being back together when she'd returned from France. Where we had parked and then walked hand in hand down to the point where diminishing heads of corn in a field alongside the lane swept up to the red brick boundary wall of the grounds of another local stately home. There, ignoring so far as was possible, the sights and sounds of other people, I had looked out across farm buildings and a herd of cows grazing in a field beyond, to the lake and its stag-headed heronry, hearing with surprise, a voice which I recognised as my own, telling Frances that I wanted to be with her always and hearing her reply that it was much too early to be promising any such commitment to each other yet. A special place. A magical place. Of course we had chosen to go there time and time again.

"It's the local knocking shop!" Phil broke into my silent reminiscence to exclaim.

"In daylight? And in a dinner hour?" I snapped back...
....
......"Hang on a minute." I broke into his story. "I'm confused now. Remind me who Phil is."

"My friend." He glared at the interruption. "The one who got me the job. I told you about him this morning."

"Yes, okay, I suppose you did." I said after a moment's thought. "It's just that I've had a break in between in which to forget details like that."

"I hope I'm not *boring* you with this story that's so easy to forget." He snapped irritably.

"Of course not." I feigned a yawn. "You are still Geoff, I take it? Even though you're dressed differently now."

"Of course I am. I've already told you that. What do you think? I'm making this up."

"And not making a very good job of it? Yes, it had crossed my mind."

"Look, do you want me to carry on?" He glared at me. "Or do you want to go back to your hedge cutting?"

"Oh carry on please." I said sarcastically, with a mock bow.

He glared at me for a moment more before going on. "I don't know where I'd got to now." He complained petulantly.

"Phil had just told you you'd been seen down the back lane to Acton Hall, and you'd replied it wouldn't be likely at that time of day." I looked at him interrogatively as a sudden thought occurred to me. "Is that still the place to take a girl round here by the way?"

"What?" He looked back at me blankly. Knocked off his stride by my sudden question.

"The back lane to Acton Hall. You said you'd been seen down there with Frances. Is that the place to take a girl if I get lucky whilst I'm here?"

"Only if you're the sort of person who does that sort of thing Pete," he said coldly. "I'm not, and I told Phil so, but he obviously didn't believe me."....................

....

......"I suppose you'd have to snatch at whatever opportunity offered if it's the only chance you get. *Is* it the only chance you get?" Phil probed.

"Mind your own business, Phil." I snapped.

"Suit yourself." He replied huffily. "I was only telling you for your own good. Maynard's claiming to have seen you together in a car with its windows steamed up and the chassis rocking from side to side."

"Maynard obviously has a vivid imagination."

"Then why present him with the opportunity to give it free rein? Can't you see the woman in the evenings for heaven's sake?"

I did, already I did, but even that wasn't enough. Frances had put herself forward to do the late shift at the gardens the day she had returned from her holiday. And though we had tried, unsuccessfully as Phil's interference had now revealed it to be, to hide our association from prying eyes by not doing the same late turns, I was always around to meet her once the shift had finished.

But what can you do for an hour at ten o'clock on a Monday or Tuesday night? Where can you go? How do you keep the sordid nature of back lanes and dark corners from despoiling what you yourself cherish and hold sacred? Frances and I had fallen in love with each other, and though we couldn't expect her husband to view the situation with equanimity if he ever found out about it, there was no reason at all for our workmates, who weren't personally involved in any way except as on-lookers, to decide to take the moral high ground the way they had, and tut-tut disapprovingly about us whenever they got the chance.

Phil, of course, claimed to have once successfully made love to one of his ladies whilst parked in his car in a car park at Sainsbury's, but I was becoming increasingly disenchanted with Phil and the double standards he lived by.

"Shouldn't mess with married women should you?" Was his breath taking response to my next attempt to extract a little sympathy from him in the face of my predicament.

"*You* do." I retorted.

"No." He shook his head firmly.

I reeled off a list of the dozen or so who sprang most instantly to mind. "You've been out with all of them to *my* certain knowledge," I challenged him, "and there may even have been others who I don't know about as well."

Phil nodded reflectively. "One or two others," he acknowledged with a complacent smile.

"So why is it suddenly so wrong for me to emulate you? What difference do you see between *you* doing it and *me* doing it?"

"Because I go out with them and nothing more," he explained sagely. "Gives them a little excitement in their lives and stimulates their barren marriages. It's what they're looking for and the service I perform for them. I never do what it is that you're doing," he added piously. "Try to break up a relationship."

"What about Diane?" I demanded indignantly. "She broke up with her husband after going out with you, didn't she?"

"Sure she did," he agreed, "but not through any action of *mine*. It was the fellow who she had after me that her husband caught her in bed with."

"And that was no fault of yours of course? That she'd gone off the rails in that way."

"It was not! Diane was a scrubber by nature. She would have had some bloke or other sooner or later whether I'd come along or not. I happened to be the first, but there was no significance in that. It could have been anyone. Might even have been you."

"No." I said firmly, and meant it.

"Why not?" He snorted, adopting a tour guide stance - in full flood now. "You like to think this thing of yours is something so special, but really you're no different from anyone else. Once Frances finds out how easy it is to cheat on her old man there'll be no stopping her. You're just showing her how to do it that's all. She'll be cheating on you too, just as quickly. You'll see."

"No!" I recoiled from the thought.

"Of course she will!" He sneered. "What do you think you have to offer her that nobody else can better in any way? Look at yourself. You're nothing special after all. And even if she *did* leave her old man for you, you'd never be able to trust her after that, now would you? What she's doing to him, she'd be certain to do to you as well sooner or later, given the opportunity."

"No." I rejected his argument a third
time, feeling, nonetheless, that I was drowning in the sea
of supposition he was conjuring up from the false prem-
ise that his knowledge of women made him an authority
on love. Of himself perhaps, I thought grimly, but never
of anyone else. "You're wrong Phil. You know nothing
about us."

"Oh get wise Geoff," he snapped. Phil was never
pleased to have his flow of rhetoric stemmed. "She's
shown herself to be available and I can understand you
wanting to take advantage of *that*. Frances is a tasty bit
of stuff right enough. But, for heaven's sake, just give
her a quick poke, and leave it at that. You're only building up trouble for yourself with all this talk of permanent
relationships and the like. Remember, it wasn't *me* whose
jaw was broken by Diane's husband."

"Smell of roses don't you?" Now it was my turn to
sneer.

"Well that's better than what *you'll* smell of if you
don't heed my advice Geoff," was his fierce rejoinder.
Then, conciliatory, exercising the charm which regularly
set female hearts aflutter. "Look, I've known you for
enough years now to know how it is you want to feel
about her but, just this once, be guided by someone with
more experience in these matters than you have. A quick
poke, like I said, if you feel that you can't live without *that*, but then call it a day. There isn't a woman *alive* who's worth all the troubles *you're* lining up for
yourself with this. Take it from me."

I didn't argue any further. What would have been
the point? For all his talk of experience, what could Phil
possibly know about Frances, for whom I often sat wait-

ing for an hour, in order to spend maybe forty minutes in her company? Getting to know the late evening voices on my car radio, presenting shows I hadn't even been aware existed until now.

Noisy, but sometimes even they were not as noisy as the pubs in which we were most likely to end up nowadays. Sipping a half of something, as we sat as close as possible to each other in the darkest corner of a bar full of teenagers, who were probably more able to achieve complete satisfaction than we were ourselves.

Phil was wrong, he had to be wrong, but he was only the first to express his disapproval of my relationship with Frances in that way." ....
....
......"There were others then?" I asked interestedly. Breaking into his story as he paused for breath.

"Oh yes there were others," he replied grimly. "My mother for one."

CHAPTER SIX

Have you ever heard of the Hypoboreans?" Geoff Truscott asked unexpectedly. Digressing, temporarily at least, it seemed, from what he had been saying before.

"Er…no - I don't think I have." I confessed, after thinking about it for a moment.

"No, I don't suppose you would have." My companion said, a shade dismissively. "Why would you, unless you were like me – lived more years than are good for you, and have spent most of them soaking up pieces of useless information like a sponge.

Well, the Hypoboreans were a long ago race with a priesthood they called the Samethoi, who the Ancient Greeks spoke very highly of, and who were followers of a god of the Underworld in the dim and distant past. A sort of early version of the Egyptian god of the Underworld, Osiris. Their role, if you believe in that sort of thing…"

"Like you do?" I put in quickly.

"Yes, like I do." He replied, almost defiantly. "Why not?" He glared at me for a moment, as if expecting further interruption, but when it didn't come, went on……..
……………………………………………………………...……
……."The role of the Samethoi was supposed to be to enter the Realms of the Dead at the time of the first frosts, and conduct the souls of anyone who had died during the year to their place of rest, and to bring back knowledge and enlightenment to the ordinary people.

At Samhain, the veil between our world and the otherworld is at its thinnest. Found in the sign of Scorpio, if you're talking astrology, Samhain rules the eighth house of death and rebirth. It's the time when we ought to be facing up to the consequences of any of our actions during the previous twelve months if we believe in an afterlife of any sort, so they don't get recorded, and then counted against us when we die. Appropriate really, that a love which began at Imbolc, and was declared at Lughnasad, should reach a crisis point at the third of the four ancient Celtic fire festivals which were still part of everyday life in this country, until only about a hundred years ago.

In Oxfordshire, an unmarried girl, armed with a borrowed scythe, was supposed to climb over the walls of a churchyard on Samhain night and cut down any hempseed plants she found growing amongst the graves, if she hoped to see the shade of her future husband lurking in the shadows there.

In other parts of the country, it was the practice for a couple to throw two nuts into a fire. If both nuts exploded then there was true love between the petitioners. If the nuts merely whistled, or whimpered, then love between the pair was dying. If one nut exploded, whilst the other simply sizzled, then one partner loved more ardently than the other.

It was supposed to be a means of divining your sweetheart's true feelings and may well have been the case. I hadn't any nuts to try in the ashes of the bonfire in the woods where the garden staff had been clearing a fallen tree the following morning which, as it turned out, was probably as well. I *did* have potatoes though, and two of these, baked in their jackets, were nicely done in time to take them up to tea later that morning. Frances, meeting me by the door, warming her hands a little uncomfortably on the cooking foil surrounding her potato as we made our way to the rest room.

We were both only too well aware that if Frances hadn't got herself transferred from seasonal staff to permanent staff recently, after a confrontation with her husband, who found her sudden career change difficult to come to terms with, our time of working together would have soon been coming to an end.

He'd put it down, I believe, to thinking she had come into contact with strong women at work, who had encouraged her to express herself as a woman, by forging an independent career path for herself. Something which women seemed to have been doing more and more since the war had brought them out of their homes and into the wider world. Little realising that it had actually been that oldest need of all, love, which had been the real reason for her seeking to stay on at Moorecroft House."

"How did she take it?" Frances asked, as we were walking along together. "You did talk to her about us didn't you?"

"Yes I did." I smiled uneasily, knowing she wouldn't like what I was about to tell her.

Phil had proved more accurate in his forecast about my relationship with my mother than he was about the one I had with Frances. Once my mother had gained a foothold in my house she *hadn't* wanted to go back to living on her own. And though, as I'd said at the time, there was nothing in my life at that moment she could upset by her presence, that had all changed in a big way once I had Frances to think about. Now my mother *was* an encumbrance, because Frances and I increasingly found ourselves wanting to be alone together, but couldn't at work for obvious reasons. And though getting it together at my house ought to have been the next step in our relationship, we couldn't meet there either, because I didn't think my mother would look too kindly on such behaviour between people who weren't married to each other, especially if one of them was her son. There had been a lot of heated discussion between Frances and me on the subject, for which reason I had now agreed to tell my mother about her, so we could meet at my house whenever we wanted.

"And?" Frances prompted.

"Not very well." I confessed.

"Oh." And there was a wealth of meaning in that single word response.

"Well did you expect that she would? I .... Oh damn!" We had arrived at the rest room to discover that, what appeared to be a quite deliberate policy on the part of our colleagues to keep us separated, was obviously still in operation. The only empty seats available to us were singles at widely spaced intervals around the room.

A snigger from Walter Maynard. An "I told you so" look from Phil. I sank back into a seat by the window to unwrap my potato and drift off into a mental reconstruction of the events of the previous evening.

Not the first time I had run over them in my mind as it happened. Probably not the tenth, eleventh, or even the twelfth. A night can be a long time when you lay unsleeping, as I had done, with little else to occupy your thoughts apart bleak ones which centred on my mother.

Her reaction had surprised me by the violence of its nature though, looking back, I don't know what, if anything, I had expected her reaction to be. Surprise certainly. Maybe even a trace of annoyance at the unexpected weakness I had shown. But understanding certainly. I had, after all, always enjoyed such a good relationship with my mother. We talked to each other, discussed things, got on well together. Such a pity then, that it was all based on a false assumption of hers about me, that I didn't have any need in my life for a woman other than her. Such a pity that I had never thought to take that into account.

"You too!" Had been her immediate reaction. "I never thought that you'd do anything like that!"

Anything like what? I gulped down a mouthful of the tea I'd just poured myself before replying. Defensive. Conciliatory. Wasting my time. "Nor did I. Nor am I. It isn't like that. Just something which happened. Something I couldn't do anything about." Did I really sound as false as Phil had when using almost identical words to me in defence of his own activities? Of course there was no common ground for comparing my one-off out-of-the-blue romance with the hydra of Phil's sexual proclivities, but that was simply my point of view. Funny how what can seem special to one person, can look so sordid to anyone not personally involved.

"Of course you could do something about it!" My mother snapped at me. "You could have kept away from her for a start."

"You don't understand." I protested. "I love her."

"A woman like that!" She snapped back even more sharply. "And somebody else's wife!"

57

As if I needed reminding of *that* fact! Wasn't it tormentedly and indelibly engraved on my brain? A woman like that though! A woman like *what*? I was about to demand what she meant, but another point had occurred to my mother before I could.

"I suppose you'll want me to get out now." She said with a sigh.

"What?" I said, feeling a bit bemused by her line of attack.

"Of this house." She glared back at me. "You'll want me to get out."

"I hadn't intended it." I replied. And I hadn't. Nothing like. "That's why I'm telling you about her," I assured her, "so we can all get together one evening."

"That was what poor Mrs Snelgrove thought *her* son was going to do." My mother went on along her own line of thought, completely ignoring the conciliatory nature of my words. "But she'd signed the deeds of her house over to him when he'd kept on at her about death duties years before, and hadn't a leg to stand on as a result. Ended up in a home, poor woman. Didn't live long afterwards. Not after he'd broken her heart. That's something you're not going to do to me." She stood as if braced against some immediate attack I might make on her. As if I was going to try to bundle her out of the house there and then.

"I never intended to," I replied stiffly, hurt by the suggestion. "This isn't the same anyway. This is *my* house. You have your own to go back to if you want to. But I hadn't thought you would."

"Well don't!" She gave my sensibilities no quarter. "The way you two are carrying on might have been over-looked during the war, when nobody really knew whether they were going to live to see the next day or not, but this….there's no war on anymore, and you've no excuse for carrying on as if there is."

"All I wanted was a place to be with Frances where we needn't be in constant fear of thugs and perverts bothering us. It isn't much to ask. Or do you want me to be murdered in a dark alley somewhere?"

"If you weren't doing what you're doing there wouldn't be any chance of it happening," came the un-compromising reply. "Bringing that woman into the house!"

"Into *my* house," I reminded her gently, "and I do have the perfect right to bring home any friend I choose."

"*Friends*, yes," she snorted, "but this! Supposing the neighbours see her?"

"Well so what if they do? She won't be carrying a placard saying 'I am a fallen woman - please stone me'."

"But they might ask me about her. What am I to say?"

"Tell them the truth. I'm not ashamed of it."

"Well I am!"

And so the battle raged on, as she attributed to me every crime she could think to lay at my door-step. Harangued me for my supposed ingrati-tude. Accused me of laughing at her behind her back.

She was hurt, and I hadn't wanted to quarrel with her, so again and again I offered her the chance of a truce, but all to no avail. My mother was adamant, and would not give her ground.

"It could have been worse you know," I observed at one stage, trying to introduce a little levity into the proceedings.

"How?" She demanded disbelievingly.

"I might have come out of the closet and told you about a man." But she would not be appeased by that.

There was only one possible line left to me, and in the end I took it reluctantly, though determined not to give way. Frances *would* be coming into our home, I told her, and it might be a good thing if on the first occasion the three of us had a cup of tea and a chat in order to get to know each other. Defusing the situation and removing the imagined threat to my mother's way of life. After all, I thought hopefully, without actually voicing the opinion, it would surely be impossible for my mother to meet Frances and not end up liking her.

It was a relief in the morning to discover that we were no longer speaking to each other, though I was too pessimistic to consider it to be anything other than a purely interim state of affairs. Give my mother the day to sit and dwell on all her real or imagined grievances and she would have plenty more ammunition with which to lash out at me later. Maybe even enough to be able to spare some for Frances, though I was being a little bit premature in worrying about that yet.

"I'm not coming."

"*What*?" Break time was over now and we were making our way back to our respective duties. Frances was slightly behind me and I paused to turn and look back at her in disbelief.

"I'm not coming." She repeated defensively. Staring me straight in the eyes defiantly.

"But I went through hell and back last night setting the scene so you *could* come to my house." I objected fiercely. "You can't just back out now."

"I can." She replied with spirit.

"Why?"

"Your mother didn't like the idea very much did she?"

"Not a lot." I admitted ruefully.

"No, and I can't blame her. Whatever must her opinion be of me? I know what my feelings about *her* would be if our positions were reversed. No. It would be too embarrassing to have to meet her under such circumstances. Sorry Geoff."

"But Frances….."

She was gone, and I was left standing there open mouthed in disbelief. Stirring myself into disconsolate movement at last I bumped into Hargreaves at the corner.

"Ah, Geoffrey. I was just coming in search of you."

"It *is* my break," I pointed out a shade irritably.

Hargreaves consulted his watch ostentatiously. "Perhaps a little more thought given to your work and less to other matters?" He nodded in the direction of the office, where Frances was to be heard clattering things about angrily.

"I do my job." I replied sharply.

"Yes," he agreed, "but only after a fashion. Do you know what someone said to me the other day? That you're too interested in walking around holding hands with that woman to do your job properly these days."

"But that simply isn't true!" I exploded.

"*Possibly* not," and the first word was very heavily emphasised. "But you must know that you're leaving yourself wide open to accusations of that kind of late.

Now I don't know just what your relationship with Frances is. Nor do I want to," he added quickly, "but if it's the cause of your hanging about in places where you aren't supposed to be when you should be working, and returning from your breaks long after you should, I want it to stop. You're a tour guide here remember. It's time that you got back to acting like one!" And recognising an exit line which couldn't be bettered, he vanished back down into the depths of the building, leaving me to follow on behind, fuming at my perceived injustice of it all.

I paid heed though to what he had been saying. Recognising the element of truth in it, however distorted it might have become within the framework of innuendo and lies, and was very circumspect about my timekeeping and work throughout the remainder of the day.

"Frances won't be coming," I announced that evening over a meal of burnt meat and underdone potatoes. My mother, usually an impeccable cook, was certainly using every means at her disposal to make her feelings plain.

"Who .... ? Oh that woman! Why isn't she?"

"Because she thinks it would be too embarrassing to meet you after all."

A sniff from my mother. "Well at least it seems she still retains *some* sense of propriety." She said, as she began to clear the table and I made my way up to my bedroom to ruminate on the injustice of life, and to wonder if I might be wrong after all."

Shaking his head as if trying to clear it of a memory of some sort, Geoff relapsed into silence..................... ...."Wrong about what?" I asked into the silence.

"Wrong about everything." He said after a minute or two more. "Especially about my expectations of what I was going to get out of this relationship with Frances.

I had always felt that if I stuck with her long enough things would eventually break the way I'd been hoping they would. I mean, she *was* the love of my life after all, and I'd been waiting for her to come into it for such a long time, I felt that now she *had* come, I only had to stick with her – with *us* - and things would eventually turn in my favour. And I was prepared to wait until she saw it too."

"To wear her down, you mean?" I asked sharply.

"No," Geoff replied coldly, suddenly going very quiet on me again, and standing looking into nothingness, as if trying to sort things out in his head before he finally answered, which he did eventually. Saying thoughtfully, "I preferred to think that just as *I* knew we were meant for each other, she would eventually come to see that too. Then she would leave her husband for me. And I was sure that she *would* do that in the end. It was just a matter of time. But until then the letters I wrote her were sometimes our only means of communication. I couldn't very well telephone Frances at home could I? In case her husband picked up the phone, or overheard the conversation. And I wasn't able to see her for very long, or very often, in the evenings at that time, or ever again, as it turned out. Just thinking about her when we were apart wasn't enough. I felt I had to be doing something *constructive* about the relationship. Something *physical* to express my feelings for her and fill the empty hours I was sometimes left with." He relapsed into silence and I picked up my hedge cutters yet again, wondering if this was the time to finally leave him to his mournful memories and get on with my work.

CHAPTER SEVEN

"Surely you were still able to see Frances during the day though? Like you used to in the beginning." I said, at last, without actually turning the cutters on. I don't know why I said it. My companion had remained sunk into silence for so long this time, it would have been the perfect time to get back to my work again. But that would have left his story unfinished. And though, at the time, I didn't really know *why* I thought it – my Grandfather getting involved again perhaps - I had the feeling, for some reason, that his story ought to be told.

"Sometimes," he said at last, after a moment or two more thought on the subject, "but not at often as I would have liked to see her. She had far too many other commitments, you see, not just me, and wasn't always able to simply drop them when she wanted to, like I could mine. Even though she generally wanted to drop hers as much as I wanted to drop mine. Or she said she did anyway."

"Did you ever find yourself feeling that the end, even if you got there, wasn't going to be worth all the ducking and diving it was taking to achieve?" I asked. Wondering if I would ever think *any* girl was worth that much anguish.

"No." He answered straight away, without apparently needing to give any thought to the reply. "*Never.* If you'd ever met Frances you wouldn't have needed to ask that. Especially during those times when we *were* out together. Because, however long or short that time was, it made all the hours when we were apart worthwhile.

"Was it difficult hitting on a places to go to, though?" I asked. "Or were there some places you went to more often than others? Like the serpentine lake in the gardens was where you said you went to thrash out any problems you had."

"Not really." He'd had to think about that for a moment as well. I seemed to be taxing his remembrance of events a bit with my questioning. "We worked on the theory that we stood more chance of being seen by someone if we went to the same place too often. Unless it was somewhere a long way from home, but then it would take us too long to get there and back and we wouldn't be able to spend much time there. It *was* nice to lose ourselves in complete anonymity and walk about hand in hand at places like that, as if we were just any other couple, though.

We did usually *meet* at the same place though, before we went off wherever it was we were going. There's a car park outside a country park down towards Hereford, which we used a lot, because not many other people do, so there wasn't much chance of us meeting up with anyone there we would rather not have had seen us. It was there I'd arranged to meet Frances one morning, so we could go off into Hereford together.........................
....
.......She was late and I was worried. Had I chosen to come to the right car park I was beginning to wonder? There were two in the vicinity, and though I was pretty sure it was the right one I had come to, it just *might* have been the other one that she'd said.

I decided to give her just a little while longer before I went off anywhere else. This wasn't our first outing and

66

she'd been twenty minutes late the time before. We'd gone for a meal in Shrewsbury that day. A place in the centre of town near the castle. Something I'd said in a bookshop we'd visited later had sparked off a tirade. "So clever aren't you? Studying for a degree, whilst I'm just a nobody who knows nothing at all."

I had been taken aback by her outburst, unsure whether to feel wounded or amused. "There's nothing to *that*," I said soberly. "*I* don't think so anyway. And I'm not actually studying for one yet am I? When I *do* finally get to go for one, *if* I do finally get to go for one, I'm sure studying for a degree will be just like any other form of hard work when you come down to it. Repetitive too. Nothing I'd put on airs about doing I promise you. I'm not like the other tour guides remember. *My* ego doesn't oblige me to go around putting on airs about anything."

"But you do. You know you do!" She'd countered earnestly. "You're always spouting off about this or that. Things I didn't even know existed. How can you have a conversation with me? No!" As I'd smiled. "I'm serious. What do you expect of me?"

"I don't know really," I'd answered lightly. "I could make you another Eliza Doolittle I suppose. Or a Trilby O'Ferrall perhaps."

"A Trilby *who*?"

"O'Ferrall. You know. Svengali and Trilby. The book by George Du Maurier. Did you know that the hat was named after that worn by the heroine in the stage version of the play?"

It had taken a lot of the rest of that afternoon, several cups of coffee, and much surreptitious hand holding in a tearoom, to convince Frances that I really hadn't been sending her up. That people studying for a degree, or even those only hoping to get to study for a degree, do, as a result of their researches, tend to collect snippets of perfectly useless information like that. Keeping them bottled up for years, sometimes, until opportunity suddenly allows them to lay a particular morsel out. Our differences over that, though, were what first gave me the idea of writing the letters to her I used to pass some of the many hours I had to fill when we were apart.

I'd been writing about Frances almost since the moment I'd first set eyes on her – mostly lyrics for my songs - then when a few lines of prose I'd penned to her once, beginning quite truthfully, "I've never written anyone a love letter before…." had been so warmly received by her, I'd found myself writing another, then another, each so progressively longer than the one which had preceded it.

Now I sometimes found myself sitting up far into the night, covering page after page of paper with words of love, as I passed the endless hours I had to get through without her, by writing down the things I would have been saying to her if only she'd been there for me to say them to.

There seemed to be so much to say. So many things to tell her about, that the small amount of time our circumstances allowed us to spend together just then went nowhere towards allowing a fraction of it free passage. What better way to spend the hours spent apart from Frances, than by keeping in touch after a fashion by writing to her in this way?

Phil, in one of the about faces I was finding to be so typical of the man, had not so long ago berated me for no longer continuing with trying to write my musical and I had to admit to myself, if not to him, that he was right. I found that I couldn't concentrate on anything so mundane anymore. Had he known what I was doing instead, though, and had he really cared, he could only have been happy about the six or eight page newsletters I was writing nowadays purely for Frances to read. Filled not only with love, but items of national and international news, topical extracts from the week's newspapers and television programmes, and reports on the more parochial events which had directly affected the two of us. Bettered only by those special moments, which for me were the best part of it, reading them out loud to Frances and seeing for myself her smile of appreciation of the words I had set down, the writing of them in my cold, lonely bedroom was a strangely warm and comforting experience for me.

I'd told Frances once that our love was more like a cottage industry than a simple romance and that wasn't so far from the truth. The trouble *was* that though the side of it involved with writing to her was flourishing, the more important one – to me at least – when we spent time together was in recession, and actually getting worse.

Tea and coffee breaks at the college were still being stage managed with an eye to making us act like strangers towards one another. Dinner breaks, already strained by Frances's need to go home to carry out various household chores, and her resentment at having to either rush them, or else leave them undone, were now positive minefields of discontent, thanks to my need to get back to work on time since Hargreaves' word in season to me, and the perverted sense of pleasure which inspired Maynard to drive down the back lane to Acton Hall from time to time, "Just to see what was doing," as he put it. Ten or fifteen minutes together were not even enough to enjoy a proper quarrel, but it was all we were managing of late. It wasn't surprising then, that those snatched moments when we *could* be together, precious as they were, were more often than not spent quarrelling over something, instead of being filled with love. That was why I had taken the time one morning to surreptitiously cut a single red rose I'd seen growing in the borders and hand to her at lunchtime. But even that hadn't been well received.

"Thank you, but what am I supposed to do with this now? Take it home so Jean can see it? I'm sorry but....Ooh!" She had absentmindedly twisted the stem of the rose between her fingers and pricked herself with it. Now she licked a spot of blood from her finger of Mercury. Seat of all sexual traits, as well as those of basic honesty and dishonesty. Simple chance perhaps, or had the thorn's deliberate piercing of that particular finger been indicative in some way? "I had to put a casserole on for this evening and then the window cleaner came and that woman from number seventeen across the road wanted to talk. You know how it is."

I didn't actually but, not wanting to spark off yet another quarrel, I allowed it to pass, saying instead, "Are you coming to my house tonight?"

She sighed. "You know how I feel about that."

"And you know that we can't go.... Oh damn! There's that bloody Maynard again!"

"No it's not."

"It looks like his car."

"Looks like his car, but isn't. Go on. What were you saying?"

"That we can't go on snatching odd moments in dark corners like this. Especially when half the world seems to know about us anyway. You'll have to come out into the open with the other half sometime."

"Will I?" She said sharply. "Why?"

"Because it's either that, or give up altogether," I answered more placidly, "and I don't think that either of us is quite ready for that as yet. I know I'm not."

"You haven't told me yet what your mother said when you told her about us."

"Nor am I going to. That was weeks ago, and she's had time to get used to the notion since. Please come round tonight. How are we ever going to get together if you don't bite the bullet and give her another chance?"

She looked down reflectively for a minute or two at the rose she was still twisting between her fingers then, "All right, I'll come. But don't expect too much of this. She might not like me."

I smiled broadly, my spirits soaring rapidly. "You come round and be your usual self and she won't be able to help but like you."

And neither could she. Her comment afterwards that Frances "seemed quite nice," might not have been much, but it was more than I could initially have dared hope for. She even stopped referring to Frances as 'That Woman'. A title about which I had gone to great pains never to show my intense irritation whenever it had been brought into use.

A victory then, but the evening had been a long one, and though not as long as the interminable age it had seemed to be to me at the time, Frances had been particularly late in heading for home, at the end of it, and Jean, her husband, who was usually in bed asleep when she got home from seeing me, was sitting up watching a late film on the television instead. Words followed, the outcome of which being that Frances deemed it wiser not to court trouble by risking a repeat until his suspicions had died down again.

"It's like being a teenager ruled by daddy," I grumbled, but I could see the point of her caution really.

"It'll only be for a week or two," she squeezed my knee encouragingly. "We can wait that little bit longer can't we?"

And so, because we had no option but to do so, we did, but there was no getting away from the fact that, whatever iniquities our fellow tour guides might believe the two of us to be guilty of, in one respect at least our relationship was still incomplete.

CHAPTER EIGHT

Having to see even less of Frances, when I hadn't thought that I saw very much of her anyway, was something I had to come to terms with very quickly, but it did make me begin to briefly wonder, for a second time, if I'd been right in my belief that we would eventually be living together as husband and wife, and that the women who'd gone before her in my life had been as wrong for me as she was right.

The time when I was going to have to present my case for being allowed to study at the college of music was getting near, now, so I gave my spare time over entirely to that instead of to her, and didn't want to be interrupted by anyone. No wonder, then, I hadn't been pleased to be disturbed by the sound of the phone ringing and to find, on lifting the receiver, that the interrupter at the other end of the line was Phil with plans of his own.

I had already been glaring at the telephone for disturbing my concentration when I had picked it up and what I heard when I did annoyed me even more. I held the receiver away from me and glared at it, as if it was in itself responsible for the words that had come from it, then put it back to my ear with what must have been a very audible sigh.

"I said are you doing anything tonight?" If my sigh was as audible as I'd hoped it was, Phil obviously chose to ignore it. "I've got a couple of women lined up if you're interested."

"I'm studying." I said, with another sigh. "And you're breaking my concentration."

"Oh you can do your studying another night," he told me easily. "You won't be able to get back to it now that your concentration's broken anyway."

"It's not quite broken Phil," I answered icily. "Not if you ring off right away. I can still pick up the thread of it, don't you worry yourself."

"But what about this woman? The one I've got lined up for you."

"What about her? What do I want with a woman? She isn't married is she?"

"No," he missed, or chose to miss, the deliberate sarcasm in my voice, "but she *is* a randy piece, I promise you. Both of them are. In fact, I was thinking we could maybe do a turnaround halfway through the evening."

My god! I thought. About the last thing I wanted in my life at the moment was two of Phil's randy women.

"What do you say?" He broke into the silence of my reverie.

"No."

"No?" He questioned in disbelief.

"No." I said again more firmly.

"Why not?"

"Well, Frances, for one thing."

"How is she ever going to find out about it as long as you don't tell her?"

"*You* might tell her."

"*Me*!" The surprise in his voice sounded almost genuine. If I hadn't known Phil as well as I did I might have believed him. "Why should *I* tell her?"

"For the same reason you'd ring up offering me shares in your randy pieces, when you know I'm already firmly committed elsewhere." I said coldly. "Now if you don't mind Phil, I'm busy. I'll see you around sometime I expect."

"Yeah…..Yeah…..Okay."

The phone at the other end clicked and I put my own phone down before returning to my writing, after a pause to reflect on how much like a record request programme life can sometimes be. I don't have that record by Tommy Bruce and the Bruisers in my collection - 'Ain't Misbehaving' I think it's called - but if I had, I might well have brought it out and played it then.

I said as much to Frances when I saw her at work the next day, but she wasn't really interested in my observation. Only in the fact that Phil had felt the necessity to offer me his spare women in the first place.

"Have you been telling him about us?" She wanted to know. "About us not getting to see each other as much as we'd like?"

"Now do you think it's very likely I'd do that?" I asked exasperatedly.

"Do you ever see Caroline?" She went off at a sudden tangent.

"Why do you ask?" I answered question with question, not at all taken by the way the conversation was going. "If you remember," he darted a look at me and I nodded my confirmation, it hadn't been *that* long ago he'd last mentioned her. Perhaps he had the suspicion I wasn't really listening at all, just pretending to humour him, in case he got violent. "Caroline had been the woman in my life before Frances came along. We had seen each other for a number of years, and I think she would have liked to have made the relationship permanent, but

75

I was too sure of the real woman, in the shape of Frances, coming along one day for that. Anyway....

"*Do* you ever see her?" Frances repeated insistently.

"Well .... yes." I answered reluctantly at last. Because I *had* gone to see Caroline. Probably because of my brief uncertainty about my relationship with Francis surviving, and the need for reassurance that what I had with her was totally different from what I'd had with Caroline.

"You didn't tell me."

"There was nothing to tell. It was only once when I was in the area where she lived and dropped in to see her for old time's sake. It was a mistake, I promise you. I found that out very quickly. Just being with her seemed funny - even after such a short time apart. Touching her would have been.... I don't know! Uncomfortable. Wrong. We talked for a while and then I came away."

"And *me*?" She wanted to know. "Did you talk about *me*?"

"No," I sighed, "I didn't talk to *her* about you either. Sorry, since you seem to think that you should form such a major part of any conversation I have with *anyone*, but what would there have been to say? I've just popped round to tell you about the woman who's replaced you in my life?"

Bizarre, considering the infrequency of our meetings at any stage of our relationship, I thought, as I drew into that familiar gravel drive, to park just beyond the laburnum tree I had planted for her a few years earlier. Wondering if I should, perhaps, have phoned to warn her of my impending arrival. In the past I hadn't always bothered, but somehow this particular separation seemed to call for a more formal approach.

You wouldn't have known it though from the smile with which she greeted me as she opened the door to my knock a few moments later. "Geoff." She brushed the hair back out of her eyes with a gloved hand. Obviously I had interrupted her in the middle of housework. "What a pleasant surprise. I didn't expect to see you so soon. Come in."

"So soon?" I echoed, following Caroline into the hall with its familiarly elusive aroma of.... polish.....air freshener? I was never really sure which, but it would always remind me of Caroline, just as bonfires took me back to summer evenings on my father's allotments, coal smoke to a cycle ride I did once to Kings Norton, and the lingering scent of perfume in my room hinted pleasantly of Frances. Caroline had never smelled of perfume I re-alised suddenly, and a little unkindly perhaps. Only of polish, or air freshener.

"Well it's only been three months since you were here last, hasn't it?" She threw over her shoulder as she led me into a sunlit room at the front of the house. "After what was said last time we met, I'd expected it to be closer to Christmas before I saw you again. *If* I saw you again. Probably when I started thinking about making the mince pies."

"Only three months since I was last here!" I echoed again, with ill-disguised surprise "It seems much longer than that somehow."

"You must have been missing me." Caroline laughed at a compliment which had really been nothing of the kind. Simply the startled realisation that so much had happened to me during the intervening period that I seemed to have lived two lifetimes at least since we had last met. "*Must* have been missing me," she emphasised, turning suddenly and giving me a long, hard look. "You've lost so much weight. You surely can't have been pining. Have you been on a diet though?"

"Of sorts I suppose," I mumbled. Not about to divulge to her the precise details of how it had been done.

"Yes, I can see now that you have," she went on brightly, still subjecting me to a close scrutiny. "Your face especially looks so much better for it. Keep on with it Geoff. The leaner look suits you. Now sit down somewhere whilst I go and make us both a cup of tea."

She left me and I looked around the room after she'd gone, marvelling that I could once have been as at home there where I now felt like a stranger, as I was in my own house. The three piece suite I had risked a hernia helping a delivery man struggle into the house with. The music centre I had rewired after the plug had gone off with a bang the previous Christmas. Even one of the ornaments on the shelf in the corner was something I had brought home for her from a holiday a year or two before. When Caroline came bustling back into the room with a tray and a bright, "I didn't bring the biscuits, because I didn't think it was fair to tempt you," I sat on the edge of a chair and sipped at my tea uncomfortably. Determined not to give anything away in conversation, whilst being only too well aware that my entire demeanour must have seemed very strange to her.

She made no comment on the fact, however, and I had adjusted enough by the time I left to be able to believe that, maybe, I had done sufficiently well to have carried it off after all.

And yet. She had telephoned me on a number of occasions afterwards, which really *was* a little unusual for Caroline since we had stopped seeing each other regularly. I had been friendly, but reserved and eventually the telephone calls had ceased. There had been a card on my birthday, which had been around the same time, and which she always remembered, but though I remembered hers too, shortly afterwards, I didn't acknowledge it in any way and she must have understood the significance of that, because after that there was nothing more. I had always made it clear to her that however irregular our relationship might seem to be, there was only ever room for one woman in my heart at a time and if another ever came along to replace her in my affections, that would be that.

I hadn't told Frances, and I wouldn't have told her now if she hadn't more or less forced the information out of me. Bloody Phil! I thought angrily. He seemed to have more and more to answer for!

It was early December and bitterly cold even for that month. The following day being Saturday, I had arranged to meet Frances in the morning for a walk in a park in Church Stretton, but somehow, instead, we found ourselves pushing our way through that familiar gap in the perimeter fence of Moorecroft House and making our way towards the track around the serpentine lake there. Hoping the cold weather would prevent anyone else from being out and about there to see us together.

Feeling guilty about Friday's fracas, I had set out early, and stopped off at a nearby florist's, intending to buy Frances a bunch of red roses to say 'sorry,' but without success.

"Christmas guv," the florist had explained to me apologetically. "The growers hold back all the red roses 'til then to get a better price for them. I can do you a nice bunch of yellow though."

I seemed to remember a hit record someone once had about a yellow rose in Texas they were going to see –Gene Autry I think it might have been – and someone else – Bobby Darin I think it was – had recently been in the charts with a song about a bunch of yellow roses, the significance of which I couldn't recall for the moment, so I settled for a single stem instead. Just as well under the circumstances, since even that wasn't very well re-ceived.

"I don't want your roses," was Frances's opening line when I offered it to her. "Nor do I want your words," she interposed warningly as I opened my mouth to speak. "There are too many of them always washing over me. You're clever Geoff. Much cleverer than me. You talk and you talk and you talk, and all the while you're putting ideas into my head I never wanted to have there. I'm not me anymore. I realise that now. You won't allow me to be. I've become just an extension of you with your constant talk, talk, talk. "No." Imperiously, as I opened my mouth again - to gulp actually, but she'd taken it that I was about to protest. "You hear me out for a change and pay attention to what I'm saying, because this is it. The end of our relationship."

I reached out my hands towards her, then let them fall back uselessly by my sides. I ought to have used them to draw Frances to me, but how could I whilst she stood looking so fiercely up at me, breathing heavily, the speech I suspected she had been practising since she got up that morning completed, temporarily run out of steam.

Why? My mind begged of me in mute entreaty, as the tongue-tied turmoil her words had made of me sought to subside.

What's brought about this change in her since yesterday? We were uneasy with each other then, were often were those days, but there had been nothing to prepare me for this surprise attack. It wasn't fair. I hadn't expected to have to fight for the survival of our relationship in this way when I'd set out to meet her that morning.

"Shall we walk?" I found my voice at last, and took control of both the situation and of Frances's arm, to guide her away from the woods towards this track, the one where you're working now," Geoff put in as a sort of aside to me, so I'd know where he was talking about, "and where we hoped no one else would be at that time of day to overlook our quarrel."

"I had a long talk with Jean last night," Frances had got her breath back now and, having deliberately freed herself from my grasp, was walking a good arms-length away from me. "He knows things aren't right between us, but he hasn't an idea what's causing it. He's trying to patch things up though and I'm.... doing…this. It's no good Geoff! It has to end. And you have to accept the fact!"

"Frances….I….I…." my voice tailed away, was torn away, tossed away by the wind. God! If I was even half as clever with words as she believed me to be, how was it I was so bereft of them now? Now when I needed them most! Accept it? *Have* to accept it! How *could* I accept what I knew would be the end not just of our love, but of everything. I was sorry for Jean, her husband, yes, but I would be far, far, sorrier for me!

We walked on and the wind threw daggers of rain against our faces, which were already numbed by the cold. So fierce we had to turn half away from it to hear or be heard, even when jet planes weren't screaming low overhead on their way back to an RAF base just over the border in Wales.

"It isn't a good relationship," Frances was insisting. We'd reached the furthest point of the perimeter circuit of the park and walked for a while in the shelter afforded by the tall poplar trees growing there. Now we were making our way back down the opposite side of the spring meadow, a wide expanse of grass which was studded with flowers in springtime, and along the bank of the serpentine lake, where it was joined by a stream which ran sluggishly from beneath gnarled and over-hanging blackthorn bushes, and the wind was against our backs at last. It was easier to talk now, but with each step we took the hole in the fence was drawing nearer and with it, it seemed, our final farewell.

"But it *could* be a good relationship! *Would* be, if you'd only give it a chance." My voice cracked on its note of increasing desperation.

"A chance!" She cut in grimly. "How many more chances do you need? Forget me! Forget us! Find someone who doesn't cause you so many problems. It's the way we have to meet that's responsible for most of them. Hole in the wall assignations like this aren't good for either of us. And I for one really can't take anymore!"

The cars were very close now. Through the gap in the chestnut fencing, past the line of willows and we would be back to them. My eyes were watering, my mind was racing, and still I was unable to come up with a single coherent thought, one word even, which might bind this woman to me for a little longer. "Frances," I groped helplessly for something to say which would win me time, "Frances I .... I…"

"My mind's made up on this Geoff!" She interrupted. "I simply can't go on spreading myself so thinly between you both. Oh damn this weather!" She lurched suddenly, as a particularly fierce gust of wind buffeted us, then clutched gratefully at the arm I put out to steady her. Our eyes met and for what seemed like an eternity we stood staring into alternative futures of togetherness, or might have beens until, subconsciously, the choice was made, and she was in my arms, weeping against my shoulder. "Oh Geoff! Geoff!" She sobbed. "What are we going to do?"

"I'll step back a bit if that will help you," I offered later, as we sat in my car, with Frances still clinging to my arm as if afraid to let it go. "Try not to make so many demands on you, or to be so disagreeable when you get caught up in family things. It'll give you some breathing space, if nothing else."

She managed a tearful little smile of acknowledgement. It wasn't really what either of us wanted, but for the moment it would have to do."………………………
……………………………………………………………
……Somewhere behind me a clock struck five and I looked around at the noise, surprised suddenly to find it was a warm summer's day in August, not a cold, frosty

one, in December, so deep into his enchanted world had Geoff Truscott dragged me.

I hadn't *touched* the hedge again, even though, when Eddie Ponting had left me there after lunch, I'd vowed not to pay Geoff anymore heed, and I could see I was going to have a lot of explaining to do if I was going to hold onto my job under *those* circumstances.

"I have to go!" I said, grabbing up my tools, and running off down the track with them towards the yard, leaving the little man standing watching me go with the strangest of expressions on his face.

CHAPTER NINE

"I thought you might have come back to see how I was getting on." I said to Eddie Ponting when I bumped into him in the bothy after I'd put away my tools, having hurried back to the yard with them after leaving Geoff Truscott in such an abrupt way. Deciding that attacking Eddie for not coming to see me again might be my best form of defence against any complaints he might have about how little work I had done.

He frowned at my presumption. "I do have other things to do you know. Besides keeping tabs on you and your friends."

"Sorry." Quickly realising I might be treading on thin ice with that form of defence, I stepped back a bit and tried to smile ingratiatingly instead.

"What does he talk about anyway?" The other gardener, Joe, was just putting on his jacket to go home. "This bloke you've been talking to."

"What do you mean?" I turned to him a bit more hopefully, giving Eddie a moment or two to cool down.

"Well you said he never stops talking." He stopped what he was doing to look at me. "What's he talking about?"

"A lot of rubbish mainly." I answered, after giving it a moment's thought. "Something he called Imbolc, which seems to be some sort of old time festival like Easter is now, someone called Ian Wallace, who he said used to be a singer, and other things that didn't make any sense at all. Not really."

"He didn't talk about anything else then?"

I thought for a minute more. He must have said more than the little I could bring to mind after a whole day of talking. "A woman mostly, I think." I said at last.

"A woman?" Joe probed interestedly.

"Yes." I replied.

"*What* woman?" He wanted to know.

"A woman he says he's in love with, I think." I replied after a moment or two mores thought about it.

"She got a name this woman he's in love with?" Eddie had come back into the room now and was preparing to go home too.

"Frances." I answered that one easily.

"Frances?" Joe probed again from behind Eddie.

"Yes."

"Frances *who*?" Eddie wanted to know.

"Oh I don't know." I said, turning to him. That was harder. Why couldn't he have been content with Frances? I had to think about that. "Some funny name. French I think he said it was."

"Not *Delamore*?" Joe asked interestedly as he was picking up his bag.

"I don't know." I looked back at Joe. "It might have been."

"*Frances* Delamore?" Eddie put in.

"Sounds about right." I considered the name. Turning back to Eddie as I did so. "Why?"

"I'm trying to remember." He knotted his brows with the effort of concentrating.

"Remember *what*?" I asked a little impatiently.

"Something about a French woman who worked here once." Eddie answered slowly, still deep in thought.

"Someone you knew?" I asked excitedly. Suddenly seeing the possibility opening up in front of me that the story the little man had spent the day telling me might not have been a complete fabrication after all.

"Oh long before *my* time." Eddie answered. Still deep in thought. "Something happened to her I think."

"What?" I wanted to know.

"I can't remember." He said exasperatingly. "Can you Joe?"

Joe shook his head. Impatient to be away. "No. But it was something not very nice." He said after a moment's thought.

"Was she one of the tour guides?" I persisted. "Geoff said she was."

"I don't know." Eddie answered. Then, after another moment's thought said, "Yes….yes, I think perhaps she was. And something happened to her."

"What?" I demanded of them both.

"I don't recall." Eddie shook his head. "But my wife will, I'm sure. I'll ask her tonight and tell you in the morning." He went silent again for a minute. "I think one of them died." He said at last.

"One of *who* died?" I asked dazedly, feeling as out of my depth with the twists and turns of *their* conversation as I had with the other man all day.

"Her, or one of the men. I can't remember which."

"*What* men?" This was getting even more confusing than listening to Geoff all day had been.

"This Frances and her man. Or was it her husband? What do you think Joe?"

"Her *husband*!" I ejaculated, but Joe had taken over the double act now.

"Yes." He said, putting on his coat and picking up his bag as he spoke. "It was like one of those emotional triangles you read about in the Sunday papers. In fact, I think it was *in* the Sunday papers."

"Which one?" I wanted to know, seeking something concrete I could actually get at to check the story.

"I don't know." He said, no longer that interested really now he was about to go home. "*All* of them probably. You'll need to nip down to the reference library and look up the paper."

"*Which* paper?"

"I don't recall. What about you Eddie?" Having handed over the baton of the conversation he made good his escape. Hurrying homeward across the yard before I could call him back.

"No, I don't know either. "Eddie looked after him in obvious annoyance at being left on his own with me like that.

"Which *year*?" I implored, as he too headed for freedom.

"I don't remember *that* either."

"Not much to take down to the library to ask about is it?" I said exasperatedly. "Anyway, it isn't likely to be open at this hour is it?"

"No, I suppose not. Never mind. I'll ask my missus tonight and be able to tell you all about it over tea tomorrow. All right?" Eddie was almost out of the door now, but paused to look back at me.

"Do you think they'll have anything about it in the guide's room?" I couldn't see myself getting a lot of sleep if I left so many questions dangling until the morning.

"What?" He said sharply, wanting to be gone.

"The guide's room. Do you think they might have anything about all this in there?"

"They might, but they might not be open now." He was out of the door now and taking his bike from the rack in the corner of the yard where it had passed the day.

"I think I'll go there anyway and see." I said - to myself really – because I could see he wasn't interested.

"Suit yourself." He said, checking the tyres for punctures. "See you in the morning." He swung his leg over the crossbar of his bike and set off across the yard after Joe.

"Okay." I said to their departing backs, then made my way to the tour guides room. Not really expecting to find anyone there, but not wanting to leave so many questions unanswered overnight. The door wasn't locked, so I pushed it open cautiously and looked in, expecting someone already inside to curtly order me to go but, as that didn't happen, I slipped carefully into a room which seemed to be devoid of any inhabitants at first glance.

There was a table in the middle of the room, with what looked like a packet of roll your own tobacco lying in the middle of it, a couple of chairs placed either side of it, a sofa off on the other side of the room and, in the far distance beyond it, an open fire against the outside wall, with two armchairs either side of it. Then I noticed a slight figure hovering in the farthest corner of the room, beyond the sofa, where she blended into the deepest of the shadows.

It was a woman with long blonde hair, still attractive despite her age, which I would have hazarded to be somewhere between thirty and forty, not really *old,* but certainly not young enough for me to be looking at her in the way I suddenly realised I was. Yet there was something about her, something about the way she looked despite her age, which made me want to look at her again. She had the sort of face which, in a different era, might have launched a thousand ships. If she *was* Frances, I could see why Geoff had been attracted to her.

"I was looking for Geoff Truscott." I said, suddenly aware that, from her point of view, I might have appeared to have been studying her in an entirely inappropriate fashion.

"Geoff *who*?" She seemed surprised that I had spoken to her, and at first I thought she wasn't going to reply. Looking back at me for a minute or two before she answered, as if uncertain whether I *had* spoken to her or not.

"Geoff Truscott." I repeated, trying not to continue to stare. 'I'm not supposed to be in here,' I thought guiltily to myself, 'she'll order me out in a minute' but she didn't, just continued looking at me for a minute or two more before answering slowly, like a foreigner speaking in a language she was unfamiliar with.

"Well he isn't here." She said, still staring at me as if I was a ghost.

"I can see that." I said, looking around the room.

"What did you want him for?" She asked disinterestedly.

"I wanted to ask him about some of the things he was telling me this morning." I replied, not ready to reveal my reasons to her yet.

"Things he'd been telling you?" She probed, showing more interest than before.

"Yes." I replied, still determined to give nothing away.

"What things?" She demanded.

"That's between him and me." I answered. "It's just that I think some of them might not be true."

"Things Geoff tells people often aren't, I'm afraid." She sighed, looking as if she might melt away altogether if I didn't do something to hold her there. "Even though, to be fair to him, he generally believes them himself."

"Are you a tour guide too?" I asked, hoping to stop her from going.

"What makes you think I might be?" She glided a hesitant step or two closer to me, making me think of a young and wary bird, weighing me up as if uncertain yet whether I was hunter or gamekeeper.

"Because you're in the tour guides rest room. Though not dressed in costume like he usually is." I said, able to subject her to a closer scrutiny now that she was emerging from the shadows, and seeing that she was dressed in an ordinary blue skirt and loose fitting sweater. "The men I work with said the tour guides don't dress up in costumes when I told them Geoff was wearing one."

"Did they?"

"You're not dressed in one though, are you?"

"No, I'm not, am I?" She looked down at herself interestedly.

"So *do* tour guides then?" I persisted.

"Do tour guides what?"

"Dress up in costumes to take visitors around. I mean," I spoke slowly, as if dealing with an idiot, "Geoff says they do, but if you're not dressed up too.... ."

"Why would it matter how I'm dressed?"

"Because you're both tour guides aren't you? You and Geoff."

"Did I say that I was?"

"I thought you did."

"Well I didn't."

"*Are* you one, though? In fact," I said, putting into words the thought I'd had when I first saw her. "Are you Frances? You must be I reckon, because you're just as he described you."

"Which question do you want me to answer first?" She looked at me with just the hint of a smile on her face. "Where Geoff is? If I'm called Frances? Or if I'm a tour guide?"

"Actually, you could also tell me why it is that Geoff is in love with you. Not that I don't think, having seen you now, that there's any reason he shouldn't be." I went on hastily.

"*Is* he in love with me?" The smile died as quickly as it had appeared, and was replaced by a frown.

"He says he is."

"Then I suppose he must be." The smile returned, to hover uncertainly for a moment, then to be replaced by the frown again. "If he is, though, why doesn't he ever come to see me anymore?"

"Doesn't he?"

"Not for a long time," she paused, as if thinking it over for a minute, "at least it seems like a long time. Perhaps it isn't. Longer than it ought to be if he really *is* as in love with me as you *say* he is though."

"He seems certain of it himself. He's been doing nothing but talk about you all day."

"That *does* sound like Geoff," she said with a smile. "If nothing else, he's a great talker. Trouble is, he sometimes seems to prefer talking about something to actually doing it. Still, I suppose that's true of most men. Even you, probably."

"I think I'm more of a listener." I contradicted her. "I've certainly been doing a lot of listening since I started working in the gardens this morning."

"We're back to Geoff aren't we?" She said with a smile. "Alright, since you seem to be so interested in us both, perhaps it's time you listened to someone else, and got a woman's point of view about my relationship with Geoff. Come over here where it will be more comfortable for you," she beckoned me towards one of the armchairs by the fire.

I hesitated, wondering why it was she was trying to get me right over there, where I'd be very close to her. "I think I'd rather sit on the sofa if it's all the same to you." I said, taking a tentative step towards it. "It looks more comfortable to me."

"Sit down there if you like, but the armchair is Geoff's favourite, and as you say you're a friend of his, I'm sure he wouldn't mind if you sat in it." She beckoned me towards it again.

For a moment more I hesitated, feeling rather like a fly being enticed into a spider's web – a black widow spider perhaps – then I went past her and flopped down into the armchair.

She sighed a long drawn out sigh, as if in contentment at me doing what she had suggested. "What did you say your name was?" She asked. And I was relieved to see she wasn't coming any nearer.

"I didn't." I repaid like with like.

"Well what is it?" She insisted.

"Peter."

"Okay Peter. Now….before we start, would you like to help yourself to a twist of that tobacco I see I left lying on the table over there?"

"I don't smoke." I started to say, then looked at the packet more closely. "Not *funny* tobacco is it?" I asked suspiciously.

"*Funny* tobacco? Why?" She demanded with the hint of a smile.

"I don't do drugs if it is."

"You don't do…." She laughed out loud at my po faced reply. "Then perhaps it's time you did Peter. Time you had a few fresh experiences. Go on." She laughed again with genuine amusement. "Don't be a party pooper *all* your life. Or do you want me to start calling you Geoff by mistake, because you're so much like him?"

I got up again and walked slowly towards the table and picked up the packet she'd spoken of, which had several ready made cigarettes in it. I sorted one out and looked at it even more suspiciously now that it was close too. "Do you want one?" I turned back and looked at her.

"I think I've gone a bit beyond reefers Peter," she said enigmatically, shaking her head.

"Reefers?" I looked from her to the cigarette and back.

"Weed, grass. Whatever you want to call it. *You* take them. Keep them for yourself if you like."

"Okay." I replied. Still not altogether happy with myself about what I was doing at her bidding. Frances certainly had a way about her though, that made you want to go along with whatever she said. I could see why she had so many men in her pocket. Me included it seemed, as I put my doubts to one side, picked up the packet and came back to the armchair with it, sorting out one of her funny cigarettes as I did.

"Good!" She applauded. "Now there ought to be a spill somewhere you can use to light it from the fire. And whilst you're over there, you can stir that up too, so we've got a bit of light, then come back over here, sit down again and I'll tell you about Geoff and me."

I did as she said, sorted out a taper, lit the reefer, and there, in that darkened room, heard a different take on the story Geoff Truscott had been regaling me with since I'd first encountered him that morning. One I thought he probably wouldn't be very happy she was sharing with me.

CHAPTER TEN

"I never really wanted to be with Geoff, you know." She began. "Did he tell you that?" She looked directly at me as she spoke.

"No," I answered after a little thought. Studying the glowing tip of the reefer uneasily. Wondering if it was already slowing down my thought processes. "He told me you were as in love with him as he was with you."

"Well I wasn't!" She snapped irritably, "but he just wouldn't accept the fact. I was happy with Jean, my husband, and would have stayed with him for life if Geoff hadn't come between us. And if he had only stepped back from me, and let me be, like I begged him to in the beginning, I would have got over him eventually and my husband need never have known. I just wasn't the sort of woman who went in for affairs, and I didn't enjoy it at all. Not at first anyway. Then I began to develop a taste for the excitement it generated in me to be – I don't know – cheating on my husband I suppose.

Being with Geoff in the beginning was like a drug I had to have my daily fix of. I got high on just thinking about being with him every day. We couldn't go on living at that pace though. We might have been acting like teenagers a lot of the time, but we were far too old to keep up that pace of life. Besides, I did still care for Jean as much as before, despite Geoff coming between us. We'd been together too many years, and shared too many experiences for me to just abandon him, despite what Geoff would have liked me to do. In the end I found myself resenting both of them for the way I was forced to divide my feelings between them, but I resented Geoff most of all. I tried to step back then and show him that he wasn't the be-all and end-all of my life.

That was why I coerced Philip into inviting me to go for a drink with him. Did Geoff tell you about that?" She looked directly at me in a very disconcerting way, and I found it hard not to drop my own eyes when she did it.

"No he didn't," I said. "He told me he warned you about Phil and you took his advice and stayed well away from him."

"Well he would say that wouldn't he? Typical man, thinking he had control of the situation, when all the while it was *me* pulling *his* strings. Philip too. He liked to think that every woman danced to his tune, but in reality it was the opposite that was the case. They were both dancing to mine." She laughed. "I've shocked you haven't I?"

"No," I answered honestly because, in truth, she hadn't. As far as I could see in my very limited as yet experience of women, that tended to be what they did when dealing with men.

"Don't lie, you might only be young, but you're still an apprentice man, even if you're not the real thing yet. Where had I got to?"

"Playing Geoff and Phil off against each other I think," I answered.

"Ah yes," she smiled again. "Well, I pretended to Geoff afterwards that I hadn't meant anything by it and I hadn't - not in the way Philip hoped and Geoff feared – but I had deliberately gone out with Philip to show Geoff that I wasn't going to always blindly toe his line. That I *did* have a mind of my own, and a life away from Moorecroft House, which didn't include him. The trouble was that, despite all that, I was only too aware in my own mind that when Geoff was close to me in those early days, the excitement of being with him was such that he had only to touch me, or look at me in a certain way, and all those good intentions went out of the window.

It was because of that, and because of him, that I first found my way to drugs you know. I know Geoff likes to tell everyone how firmly against anyone using drugs he is, but it was because of him, and my need for him, that I started experimenting with them myself. First to find one which would lessen my natural reluctance to get involved in an affair with anyone in the first place, and then one which would keep me going through all the extra demands - both physical and emotional – our relationship threw at me once it was in full swing.

In the beginning, we'd snatched every moment of the day we could possibly spend together, but when we'd been seeing each other for a while and had got things arranged so we could meet each other at night sometimes, we stopped doing that. We also stopped working on the same days as each other, in the hope that this might put our colleagues off the scent, but that turned out to be a forlorn hope.

Despite that, we still didn't give up the dinnertimes when we got together, though. They were much too important to both of us at that time to curtail them in any way. Instead, we arranged our days in such a way that whichever one of us wasn't working could be close at hand to the pub, or park, or whatever, where we were going to meet, then go off on their own to do other

things with the day once the one of us who *was* working
had gone back to work......................................
....
.......On a Thursday a few months into the relationship,
we'd arranged to be meeting for lunch at the Wheatsheaf
a pub in a village a few miles from Moorcroft House. I
was working that day, but Geoff had taken time off for
his studies. We'd arranged for him to meet me in the pub
and then go on to a library somewhere to look things up.
He'd got there early, because he was impatient to see
me, he told me later. But, because I didn't want him to
overlook the vibes I was trying to send out, that I wasn't
happy with the way things were going between us, I was
both deliberately late getting to the rendezvous and deliberately curt with him when he spoke to me after I'd
got there. I made a point of not touching my food, hardly
tasted my coffee, and suggested that that evening we
should meet in a pub down by the river in Ludlow, rather
than going to his house as had been originally agreed.
There, putting on an act of staring out of the windscreen
rather than looking at him, I told him that I'd been for a
drink in the pub with Philip at dinnertime.

I could sense Geoff trying to get his head around the
bombshell I felt sure I'd just exploded inside it, and sat
quietly awaking his reaction. Which was much calmer
and more considered than I had expected. "You were
with me at dinnertime," he contradicted after a moment's
thought.

"No," I insisted, "before that. I was late getting there
remember? Well that was why."

And that, it probably occurred to him, after a further
moment or two of thought, had also been why I had been

so sharp with him. And that had also been why he had sat there for an hour waiting for me and.... "Why Phil for god's sake?" He wanted to know.

"We'd been down to the farm to show some visitors the new lambs," I explained, trotting out the story I'd been practicing and perfecting all afternoon, until I felt it was in a form which would annoy him most. "One of the groups which was supposed to be coming didn't show up and we finished early. Philip suggested popping into the pub next door. It was only a drink!" I said firmly, feeling the waves of disapproval I was getting from him. Glad my efforts with my story hadn't been wasted.

"But with Phil!"

"It was a warm day." I rolled out the story I'd been practising. One I thought would cause Geoff the most annoyance. "So pleasant there. Philip had been pointing out to me where the first primroses were showing around the pond they enlarged last autumn and telling me what they hoped to do there this year. It seemed a reasonable thing to carry on the conversation sitting out in the beer garden. There wasn't anything wrong in it. I simply had a drink with him."

"Yes, whilst I was sitting like a wally waiting for you to turn up," Geoff pointed out, his mind probably back in those woods with the primroses, wondering if either of us were aware that in the language of flowers they spoke of emotional involvement saying, 'I may learn to love you, it is too soon to tell'. *I* certainly did. You couldn't have a relationship with Geoff without picking up titbits of information like that about things, which was why I'd mentioned them. Philip also did I imagined. He was devious enough for that. Probably had them planted for that purpose, though not specifically for use against me.

"I didn't realise what the time was until the clock on the church struck the hour. Then I had to just drop everything and leave Philip to tidy up. I still had a boot full of equipment to unload in the yard before I could get across to you. I'm sorry Geoff!"

He stroked my hair, brushed my ear with his lips and held me in silence. As I said, it had only been a drink. The trouble was, from Geoff's point of view, that it had been with Philip and I knew he felt betrayed!

We went our separate ways shortly after that, without having made up at all, and I drove home slowly. Taking care not to wake Jean when I got into bed. I didn't expect to be sleeping very well that night, or at any time until the problem I'd manufactured between Geoff and me was sorted out, but I was growing used to insomnia by that stage of our relationship, and was in need of some time in which to think.

A mistake, admittedly, where emotional matters are concerned. The more you dwell on a minor occurrence, the swifter it grows into a major obstacle out of all proportion to its true significance. Both Geoff and I needed to have been together at that point, to thrash out the parameters of our relationship in open argument, until we came to an agreement. One which suited me at least, if not him. That had been the whole point of the situation I had engineered between us.

Unfortunately, one of the big drawbacks of a relationship like ours was that we simply couldn't be available to each other at the drop of a hat when we needed to be. However unsatisfactory we found it, this was something we were each going to have to work out alone.

I turned out the light, pulled back the curtains and stood for a moment looking up at a new moon half hidden by the heads of the tall trees across the road. I watched a fox slink across the lawn below, probably off to help itself to someone's chickens, then disappear again into the shadows. I flopped into bed and a very uneasy sleep.

Geoff arrived as deliberately late for our tryst the following dinnertime, as I'd been the day before, but in his case it was the result of supressed anger, not design, as it had been with me. We'd arranged to meet at the Queen's Head, a not very well frequented pub in a village a mile or two away from Moorecroft House, where we could usually expect to be free from observers of any sort. I tried to feign brightness when I first saw him, but knew him well enough by then to be aware that poor timekeeping on his part was almost always a sign of discontent. "I thought we'd settled this last night," I broke into the silence which lay malignantly over us.

"Last night I hadn't had time to think about it." He answered shortly.

"And now?" I prompted.

"Now I have." We lapsed back into silence and I fiddled moodily with my glass.

"It was only a drink for god's sake!" My sudden explosion must have set his teeth on edge. It certainly caused an old man at the next table to jerk his drink down the front of his jacket. "I wasn't offering Philip my body."

"To Phil it'll mean the same." He snapped back in his turn. "I can almost hear him crowing over it now. A moral victory he'll be calling it as soon as he gets the chance. I don't understand you Frances," he went on reproachfully. "I told you what Phil was like. I told you what he thinks about women. I told you what he said about you in particular. Now at the drop of a hat you're standing me up to go for a drink with him. Yes you are." He beat down my protest before I'd had chance to register it. "Whilst I'm sitting inside the Wheatsheaf worrying in case anything's happened to you because you're so late, you're sitting outside the Black Dog with him."

"Don't you think you're blowing this whole thing up out of all proportion?" I asked. Knowing that this was the perfect opportunity for me to put him straight about my real reasons for going for a drink with his friend, and to do some hard negotiating, which would put me in the driver's seat in our relationship, but somehow baulking at making that move.

"No," He shook his head adamantly. "I know Phil."

"And what's that supposed to mean?" It was my turn to draw myself up coldly.

"What I say." He scowled.

"That Philip has only to crook a finger and I'll come running?"

"That Phil thinks he has only to crook a finger and *any* woman will come running."

"Me included. That *is* what you're saying?"

"I'm saying only that Phil will see it that way. And he will, believe me. I don't doubt you Frances. I just wish you hadn't given Phil grounds for justifying his opinion of you."

"Can I help what goes on in men's minds without any encouragement from me?" I said icily. "And despite your reservations, I shall continue to drink with whoever I chose to, whenever I want to. I'm not going to be tied down because of this."

"Fine." He snapped back. "Just don't include me on it when you're making up your list of who to drink with!"

We returned to icy silence and the old man at the next table righted the glass he'd spent the previous ten minutes holding down. I stared at the ceiling, at the wall, at the cigarette machine, at the back of a girl talking into a phone in an alcove across from where we were sitting, at anyone and anything which might drag my mind away from its uncomfortable awareness of the close proximity of Geoff's hand to mine, where it rested disconsolately on the bench seat.

Slide it along, I urged him silently, and touch me. Stretch out a little finger almost and I'm within reach. Weakness though. That would be weakness. Unacceptable behaviour for a man, I could sense him thinking. Lacking in pride. Let her be the one to make the first move, I was sure he was thinking now, when he lifted his hand and carefully placed it over mine, and I knew I had won. He was capitulating. I let him stew for a moment more before I gripped his fingers and let him caress mine.

"Why do we bother?" He said at last. "We know we've got to make it up eventually. Quarrelling with each other is such a pointless waste of time." He leaned forward and nuzzled my ear with his nose.

"Do you remember that friend of mine, Marjorie, who I told you about?" I asked, and it must have seemed a funny sort of response to what we had just been saying.

"The one you used to go to your book club with?" Geoff buried his nose in the nape of my neck. "Yeah."

"Well she just walked past whilst you were sitting there stroking my hand, looked straight at us, and I had to blank her."

He sat up hurriedly and looked around the bar. "Where is she now?"

"Gone," I answered briefly. "She was just on her way out."

"I thought we only used this pub because no one we knew ever came here." Geoff said with a sigh. "Will it matter that your friend had to come in here and see us?"

"Not so long as she doesn't tell Jean about it," was my uneasy reply.

"Is she likely to?"

"I shouldn't think so. There's no reason why she should. She *does* know a lot of other people we both know though, and there's no telling how these things are likely to get about."

It was just one more charge for Geoff to lie at Philip's door when he eventually ran him to ground in the public bar of the Pig and Whistle the following evening.

"Oh hello." Philip didn't seem particularly pleased to see Geoff, he told me later, but Geoff could understand that. Under the circumstances it was hardly surprising. The more so after he'd sat beside him unspeaking for the first quarter of an hour.

"I went for a drink with Frances the other day." Having fidgeted uncomfortably in his seat since Geoff had joined him, Philip finally broke the silence between them, but more in the manner of a man making a confession, than the self satisfied swagger Geoff had expected from him.

"I know," Geoff answered shortly. "She told me you'd been."

"I wouldn't have suggested it if I'd known you were waiting for her," Philip said piously. "I mean, I didn't know she was meeting you."

"That much was obvious Phil," Geoff assured him quietly.

"What do you mean?" He grew still more agitated when Geoff didn't answer him immediately. "What do you mean? It was only a drink. I didn't mean anything by it."

Geoff said he looked Philip up and down very slowly without speaking at first. Just to turn the screw a little. "We've been friends for a long time, Phil," he said to him at last, "and I think I know you inside out by now. You've never in your life not meant anything by it where a woman was concerned, so don't try telling me your stories!" The hand with which he held his glass shook as he lifted it to his lips. He hadn't realised, until then, just how angry he *was* about all of this.

Philip must have noticed it too. "I won't go for a drink with her again Geoff, I promise you," he patted his knee reassuringly.

"Don't!" Geoff snapped. "Now, shall we change the subject?" And they did...
....

.......Of course, that could still have signalled the end of all that had been good between us, if Geoff had allowed Philip's warnings about not trusting me during the early days of our being together to play on his mind. Or even if what I, myself, had once said to him, that, as time went by, he'd feel less and less able to trust me, until the day came when he threw all that I'd done because of us back in my face, had been even halfway true.

It never seemed to occur to Geoff not to trust me, though. The idea that I was betraying anyone by being with him, was not one with which he seemed able to concur. In *his* eyes, Jean was somehow entirely incidental to us. He said he respected my feelings in regard to him, but that was all. Didn't hate him. Didn't *envy* him. Why should he? Geoff was, after all, he believed, the one who held my heart. Which was why he was so easy to manipulate if ever I chose to pull the wool over his eyes. And why he couldn't see my entirely different outlook on things, that I already had one husband and didn't want another and that he just might drive me away if he continued to act as if *he* was my husband too.

"Do you understand that?" She asked suddenly. Fixing me with those soulful eyes of hers. "Why I should feel that way?"

"Of course," I lied in response. Wishing she'd leave me be to listen, or not listen, as the fancy took me, as Geoff had done when *he* was telling *his* story.

CHAPTER ELEVEN

Frances Delamore continued studying me for a minute or two more, and I had the feeling she was weighing up in her mind whether my quick answer was a lie or not. Just as what she had been saying to most of the men of her acquaintance, as far as I could see, me included, probably, seemed to have been a *succession* of lies. She didn't make any comment along those lines, though. Just carried on with her story...
....
..........."Geoff could probably tell you if it's so or not - he's the one with the encyclopaedic mind - but I think it was Sir Thomas Browne who said of sex that he would be content to 'procreate like trees' and wished that 'there were any way to perpetuate the world without this trivial and vulgar way of union'. At which point Geoff would add in that way he has of praising my attractions to the high heavens, that Sir Thomas Browne was a philosopher born hundreds of years too soon to fall under my spell, so could, perhaps, be forgiven his harsh dismissal of one of life's most beautiful experiences.

Love complete in every form and in every character. Geoff and I had finally been able to get to meet together at his house on a regular basis, convince his mother that what we were doing in that upstairs room of his was reading a book together, or listening to music together, and were just beginning to revel in full knowledge of each other's bodies when, without warning, the opportunity to do so was snatched away again.

"If she really wanted to be with you she'd find a way." Philip, who had recovered his aplomb as well as his cynical attitude towards life once the storm of my creating was over, had passed judgement only a week or two earlier, but Geoff said he had refused to be drawn on the subject at all.

"I shall never leave Jean," I had assured Geoff once when he had been pressing me too hard during the earliest days of our love affair. "Not unless I could be certain that he no longer needed me. Besides, your mother's far too old now to be made to go back and live on her own again." And in those few words the parameters of our relationship had been laid down for all time.

Geoff didn't argue with what I'd said. He'd found out long before that it was useless to try to change my mind once it was made up to anything. Besides, I sometimes suspected that when he'd originally pursued me with the object of winning my love, he hadn't really expected to be so successful at it, certainly not so quickly. Having made me his so to speak though, the next natural move for us should have been to set up home together, but since I said I wouldn't do that, he either had to insist and risk breaking our relationship into little pieces if I still wouldn't go with him and leave Jean, or cut his own losses and go off with someone else.

I hoped he wouldn't do that, but I was prepared to accept it if he did, because I was committed to my intention never to leave Jean. Geoff did seem prepared to wait for me until 'hell froze over', as I'd heard it described in a popular song recently, but the winter we went through hadn't been anything like as cold as all that. Besides, though there might be times when Geoff felt he was only living half a life without me constantly by his side to share it, I was the one leading the more difficult double life.

"I don't lie to Jean," I told Geoff once, in search of his understanding. "He simply never asks me where I've been. What he thinks I do when I go out I have no idea. Maybe he never ever considers it at all." Geoff nodded sympathetically and wondered, I hope, how it could be possible for someone with so much opportunity to be with me, to always be leaving me to my own devices, whilst he, who wanted to share every available minute with me, was forced, instead, to spend more and more hours alone.

Philip would undoubtedly have had plenty more to say on the subject had he been given the opportunity to do so. Though the fact seemed to be a long time registering, Geoff was ignoring any attempts to open discussion on it that he made.

Instead, he spent time with me whenever he could, and passed those hours when we had to be apart, either writing those interminable letters of his he was always reading out loud to me, when I would have much rather have been doing other more physical things with him, and which I had such trouble hiding from Jean when I took them home, or else studying towards his degree. The time of the presentation he had to do if he was to get onto the course at the Royal School of Music, was now drawing very near.

I spent a lot of the hours when we were apart wondering if, should we ever be able to live together as he wanted, he would become like most other men seemed to be. Every other woman I knew said that the men in their lives, however ardently they had courted them before they were married, reverted to type once that ring was on the woman's finger. For us that would mean an end to the days out together I enjoyed. No more walks. No more romantic meals. Much as I loved Jean, my husband, it has to be said that even he had stopped going out with me socially once we were married.

A woman I knew once had a friend whose husband was very loving and regularly wrote poems to her. She showed them off proudly to her friends, including the one who was telling me the story, and behind her back they laughed at his expense.

What would they have made of all the things Geoff wrote about me I wondered? Not to mention the letters, which now ran to so many pages I had been obliged to return the first two volumes to him for safe keeping, as they took up so much space, risk of discovery was imminent.

No, I thought smugly, I had Geoff where I wanted him now, and *he* wasn't going to change. Not unless I wanted him to. Nor did he, as the two of us got on with our lives within an aura of love and that same sense of invulnerability which probably characterises lemmings just before they throw themselves off a cliff.

We didn't even heed the warning which life gave us when we were walking back from the shop in the village near Moorecroft House one afternoon, blatantly holding hands. I had stopped to read a notice about a jumble sale on the village noticeboard, whilst Geoff had wandered on a little way to examine a lichen growing on the churchyard wall.

Looking along the wall to see if any other types of lichen were visible besides the common limestone one, he told me afterwards, his attention was drawn by the vague notion that he had recognised the back of the last of a line of cars which had just driven past. Forcing his mind away from its attempt to recall the level of sulphur dioxide necessary to prevent lichens growing, he realised with a start just why. It was a car I sometimes drove to our rendezvous together, but which Jean was using that day. Geoff had followed along behind it many a time after we'd seen each other at night.

How slowly had Jean been coming up the road behind us? The questions began to tumble over each other to be asked once realisation set in. Had he seen the two of us whilst we were walking along still holding hands? Had he even noticed me standing in that doorway at all? The answers to the latter two questions eventually being revealed to be no and no we breathed a concerted sigh of relief, agreed to be a little more circumspect about public displays of affection in future, and promptly forgot the whole thing.

Not for long though. Only for about a fortnight, no more. Then life gave us a second, harder, nudge, when Jean started to question me about where I was going to one evening, just as I was going out for a rendezvous with Geoff. Why he had I didn't know, but though I hoped I had put his mind at rest with the hastily fabricated story I'd told him, it had left me worried once I was out, that he might not really have believed my story, and could be following me in our other car to see if I actually went where I said I was going.

We had planned to go to the cinema in Shrewsbury, where they were showing a film Geoff particularly wanted to see, so when I said I didn't want to do that after all, Geoff wanted to know why.

"I don't know," I replied uneasily. "It's Jean. I've never seen him like it before. The mood he's in I ought not to have come out at all, but I knew you'd be waiting for me."

"I'd have understood," Geoff assured me. "I've always told you that. What shall we do though? Do you want to go straight back home?"

I hesitated for a moment before shaking my head. "No. Just drive somewhere. Anywhere. Keep an eye in the mirror though."

"Why?" Geoff glanced nervously over his shoulder. "You don't think he's followed you do you?"

"No....Perhaps .... Oh I don't know! How could I possibly know what he's likely to do? How does anyone know what someone else is going to do under *these* circumstances? I thought I knew him. Now, though, I'm not so sure."

We drove off into a painful evening, with me so edgy my edginess couldn't help but communicate itself to Geoff.

"How about Ludlow? We could walk down by the river," he suggested after we'd been driving around aimlessly for a while.

"Anywhere. Just drive." I answered distractedly. "And don't forget to look in the mirror."

He didn't, but didn't see anything untoward in it, even though we'd driven around the town twice to be sure we weren't being followed before stopping in an out of the way parking area round the back of the castle.

It allowed us to go out through the trees and across the road to the water without having to use main thoroughfares. "This is silly!" Geoff said, but I wasn't really listening, just looking everywhere all the while.

"How about a drink?" Geoff suggested when it had grown too dark for comfortable walking and the lights of an ancient pub beckoned invitingly.

"I think I ought to go home really," I answered, but I looked at my watch, and it was still only half past eight.

"Won't that look as odd now as turning up very late?" Geoff pointed out thoughtfully. "You don't normally get in until after midnight these days."

"All right," I agreed, "perhaps we *had* better give it another half hour. Then I *will* have to go home. I could say that I've got a headache if he asks why. It wouldn't be so far from the truth."

He led the way to a pub which would probably have been very pleasant to drink in under different circumstances, if every set of headlights slowing down on the road outside hadn't seemed to be nemesis bearing down on us, every shadow an angry husband waiting to leap out and bring our digressions to account.

"We *did* ought to go now," I said shortly and, though it seemed as if we'd hardly flopped into the corner seat, Geoff swallowed the remainder of his drink, and was ready to follow when I hurried out, leaving my own glass untouched.

"I'm sorry about this," I started to apologise as we retraced our steps to the car park, but Geoff stopped me by kissing the words away.

"We're in this together, Frances." He said as we stopped beside my waiting car. "See you remember that." I scrambled in and was gone.

The night passed slowly for Geoff, he told me later, though he did eventually sleep after a fashion. Disturbed by dreams of relentless pursuit by something he could sense, but not see. Morning, came at last, however, and he hurried into work. Catching up with me before I'd even had time to get out of the car. "Well?" He demanded, as I sat looking back at him through my wound-down window. "What happened when you got home?"

"Nothing." I smiled up at him and started to get out of the car. Speaking all the while. "He was in bed asleep when I got home." The dark patches under my eyes I'd seen when I'd looked in the mirror before I came out, I was sure, revealed more to Geoff than any words of mine were able to do.

"A relief?" He prompted.

"A definite relief," I smiled.

"So it was a false alarm after all?"

"I don't know about that." My smile again faded into a worried frown. "I hope so but.... You never saw him. He was like..." We'd been walking into the kitchen area together as we were talking, and in front of us could see..."Like a pressure cooker about to explode. I'll be happier in a week or two if nothing's happened by then, but I certainly don't think that we've heard the last of this yet. I won't be able to see you in the evenings until it's blown over anyway. I'm sorry, but it would be taking just too much of a chance."

Geoff sighed, but accepted that there was nothing he could do about it except agree to what I said. After all, who could know my husband's mind better than I did? And I can't ever have appeared so nervous about anything to him before.

And there had been a good reason for that too, as things turned out. The explosion only being delayed for two more days before Jean confronted me with charges of infidelity I strenuously denied.

"I won't mention your name if it comes to it," I promised over the disconsolate cup of coffee we had out on the patio together later that morning. Neither of us being able to face the enforced intimacy of the rest room under the circumstances.

"You'd better, because I'll be standing by you if it does." He contradicted firmly, "but where does he think that you've met someone else?"

"He doesn't seem to know that. It's just a vague notion he has that something isn't right. I don't really go anywhere much apart from here," I replied. "And the pictures I paint of my delightful colleagues would hardly cause anyone to believe I might be secretly in love with one of them."

"So what happens now?" Geoff asked uneasily.

"I don't know." I answered in the same tone. "It's what *he* does next that governs what *we* do, I'm afraid. What really worries me is if he starts to investigate my comings and goings further and finds that this is the only place I *could* have met anyone.

We've been too clever by far in all of this Geoff. Staying out later and later and thinking that he just went off to sleep without noticing anything, and all the while he's been sitting alone each evening, turning things over and over again in his mind, brooding on what kind of a wife I've become.

My god, when I think of it! What a terrible person I must be! Evil. I've ruined *his* life and now I'm ruining *yours*. All for my own selfish ends!"

"Don't talk stupid Frances," Geoff cut in angrily. "You haven't ruined *anyone's* life as yet. I can take care of myself, and let's face it, if Jean had taken more notice of you in the past, you wouldn't be here with me now. It's as much *his* fault as it is *mine.* As much *my* fault as anybody's. What was his attitude this morning anyway? Did you see him at all?"

"Apologetic. Almost tearfully so. I think I preferred it when he was angry. At least I felt less guilty about things. When I'll ever be able to see you again in the evenings I really don't know, though. Not for a long time I shouldn't think."

But in that I was wrong, because only a further fortnight had elapsed before I searched Geoff out one morning to ask in disbelief, "Do you know what Jean was trying to find out last night?"

"No. What?"

"Why I don't go out anymore. Can you believe the man? All that uproar because I *did*, and now he's complaining because I *don't*."

"He'd probably forgotten what it was like having you home all the while," Geoff said facetiously. "Have you been hogging the television these past few weeks?"

"Be serious Geoff," I frowned. "What do you think I ought to do?"

"Go out more if that what the man wants you to do," Geoff recommended, and *my* horizons brightened considerably too.

"You would say that!"

"Then why ask me? What do *you* think you should do?"

I pulled a face. "Go out I suppose. But I'll find some classes I can go to first and I won't be staying out late after them. It'll mean less time for us to be together, of course, but we can't go on taking the chances we've been taking 'til now."

"Doesn't *everything* in life these days seem to lead to us spending less time together?" Geoff reflected philosophically

"But?" I prompted. Because the tone of his voice seemed to require a 'but' from me.

He shrugged. "If I wasn't so sure that there's a future for us beyond all this, I'd find myself beginning to doubt it. Just make sure that you never take Jean for granted again that's all, because if anything happens to restrict out time together any further, I shall be having to give back some of the time we've already had."...........
....
........"Did he?" I asked into a pause in her account of things. Feeling Frances required more of a display of interest in what she was saying than Geoff did. Probably, as I came to discover when I got older and more experienced in life, because she was a woman.

"Did *who* do *what*?" She looked back at me a bit blankly. Obviously *not* expecting to have her train of thought interrupted like that.

"Did your husband restrict your time together anymore?"

She gave the question her full attention before replying. "I don't think so." She said at last.

"But you're not sure?"

"I'm not sure that we had enough time left." She said reflectively.

"Time for what?" Maybe it was something about *me*, but I was beginning to find talking to her even harder than talking to Geoff Truscott had been. "I don't understand."

Frances looked at me again with that enigmatic expression of hers and smiled sadly. "Let me finish telling you my story," she said, "and then perhaps you will."

CHAPTER TWELVE

I nodded my agreement to that, and Frances, after having suddenly started like a young hind startled by a threat of some sort it had caught a glimpse of out of the corner of its eye, turned and deliberately stared across the room towards the settee at something *she* could apparently see, but which was invisible to me. Then, after continuing to stare warily in that direction for a few more minutes, turned back to me and carried on with her account..

....
......"It was about that time when I started to experiment more with the drugs I was taking, to try to find one which would keep me going during the more hectic moments of the lifestyle I was leading. And it *was* a hectic lifestyle, in more ways than one.

I'd been reading somewhere about the drug the gays in America were using at the time – methamphetamine – which increases people's sexual stamina, and gives users a feeling of well-being and of being strong and full of energy. I couldn't get my hands on it at the time though, so I tried taking amphetamines instead. Similar in their effects, and much easier to get hold of, because you can get a doctor to prescribe them for you if you can convince him you're suffering from one of the disorders they treat with them, and I managed to get mine to believe that I had attention deficit hyperactivity disorder, so that was all right.

The trouble is, that if you use them in too higher doses, or for too long, it can lead to a lot of side effects. Headaches, mood changes or behavioural disorders amongst other things, which were the main effects – noticeable ones anyway – that the ones I took had on me. I thought it was worth it though – at first anyway – because it certainly helped me to lead the double life I was leading more easily. Or, perhaps, the drugs just stopped me from bothering about it at all. Whichever it was, it worked for *me.*

Apart from the mood swings I wasn't altogether sure they was responsible for, or the headaches I got from time to time when I was coming off of them, or needed an extra dose or two of them to get me through, I thought taking them was worth it in the long run, because the amphetamines kept me going longer than I would have able to keep going if I hadn't been taking them.

As he was so firmly against any sort of drugs, I didn't tell Geoff about the drugs I was taking, even though I firmly believed it was his fault I had ever had the need to take drugs in the first place.

There was very little I ever held back on telling him about during our time together, but there were a few things I *couldn't* share with and so never did. One of them was the fact that I would be going on holiday with Jean that summer. And I held back on sharing *that* piece of information until it was almost time for the plane to be taking off with us aboard. What was more to the point, from Geoff's point of view, was that I didn't tell him that Jean and I were going to be away during the week in which the anniversary of Geoff and me first getting together fell either.

This, as I firmly maintained to Geoff, when I *had* to tell him about it in the end, was because he became so disagreeable and impossible to be with the moment I passed on such information, I always left it until the last possible moment to tell him I was going to be involved with family business of any sort, rather than seeing him, in order to stave off his sulking about it for as long as I could. Geoff, who maintained that he never sulked, but simply went very quiet on occasions, countered that he responded much better when being treated as an adult and allowed the maximum amount of time to come to terms with any impending separation, and if I believed otherwise I must be confusing him with someone else.

His eyes narrowed in that familiar way of his, which always signifies maximum annoyance, when I told him I was going to be away. We were outside on the patio enjoying our afternoon tea at the time, having forsaken the tea room during a spell of warm weather. We'd carried a couple of armchairs out there to sit on, and Geoff had just raised what he thought was the timely question of what we would be doing to celebrate our anniversary, and had been told in response that there was to be no anniversary celebration for us, because I would be going away on holiday with Jean that same week instead.

"If he wants to go on holiday then, what am I supposed to do about it?" I had responded sarcastically to Geoff when he complained. "Tell him to go on his own?"

"Why not?" He retorted moodily. "He wouldn't be entirely on his own would he? Not if there's supposed to be a group of you going."

"And what do you think I should give as my reason for staying home?" I demanded belligerently.

"Tell him you've got a headache," Geoff suggested, a little unwisely under the circumstances.

"Make one up like I usually do you mean?" I snapped back.

"I didn't mean..." Geoff was instantly sorry. "I. . ."

"So you can fake the sympathy you're always professing?" I gave him no chance to go on. Getting up angrily from my chair and tossing most of my cup of tea into the bushes.

"Frances I...." Geoff followed suit and tossed the remains of his own tea over the edge of the balcony onto the bushes below. "Oh sod it!" He rose angrily from *his* chair too. "Have it your own way if that's how you want it to be." He stormed off and I watched him go before making my own angry way to meet the visitors I was supposed to be showing around the gardens.

So we went our separate ways and carefully ignored each other and, yes, it was just like 'Passing Strangers', which we both have in our separate collections, sung by Billy Eckstein and Sarah Vaughan. And all the while my holiday, when we wouldn't be able to see each other for a couple of weeks, was getting closer, and here we were wasting precious moments in foolish acrimony yet again.

I don't think you need to ask me how I know this, but I believe it was the Latin poet, Terence, who lived in Carthage a century or two before Christ, who caught it best with his *'Amantium irae amoris integration est'* which, roughly translated, means that lovers quarrels are the renewal of love. Try telling that to them whilst any disagreement is still in full spate, though. We were probably both equally in the wrong, and we knew it, but neither of us was prepared to give way.

"Any idea where Geoff is?" One of the part time tour guides came up to me as I was checking the day's rota.

"Tried by the serpentine canal?" I hazarded, marvelling at the degree of acceptance which had come with the realisation by some of our colleagues at least, that we were a convenient means of communication with each other as a rule, but wondering how best to report that, for the moment, the lines of communication were down.

"Can you help me catch a pig?" Hargreaves towered above me as I stood gazing forlornly across the lawn to the point in the woods where Geoff had just disappeared from my view.

"A pig?" I repeated, startled out of my apathy. "But we haven't got a pig."

"Tell that to Walter," the senior tour guide replied grimly. "He inadvertently let it out of someone's trailer in the car park and got bowled over trying to get it back."

I felt my mood brighten considerably. A pig which bowled Walter Maynard over couldn't be all bad. Just wait until I told Geoff, I thought, then remembered, and the blackness came down again. Damn this silly quarrel! I hurried off to join the posse which wasn't needed. Maynard, armed with a bag of pig nuts, had gone back and sorted out his own mess.

If all these people had been around last summer when our romance was just getting under way, it wouldn't even have had a chance of getting off the ground, I thought unhappily. Even Hargreaves had been there that day. I hadn't minded when he'd called me into his office for a get together at tea time. At least that had been better than spending it alone.

"Are you happy?" Philip asked me, when he could see full well that I was anything but.

"Working here, why shouldn't I be?" I replied sarcastically.

"No problems of any sort?" He'd avoided being seen talking to me since Geoff's admonition to him, but we both knew what it was he was really asking. "Nothing you want to share with me?"

Not really, though you could share with me who the source who's keeping you informed of the state of our love life is, I thought darkly, but merely shook my head. "How's Leslie?" I enquired in order to divert him, and spent the next hour listening to a racy account of his weekend with the most recent of his ever increasing band.

"Women are like buses," Philip had remarked once within my hearing. "Miss one and there's bound to be another along soon."

Yes, with its seats slashed, and graffiti all over the windows, knowing some of yours I've seen, I thought. Wondering at the same time why it was Geoff never responded verbally to Philip's veiled attacks on our differing way of life. Breeding probably I opined complacently. Or a case of sticks and stones - though that really depended on who the words were said by, as to whether or not they could hurt me at all.

Not by Philip, that was certain. Geoff though.... he could even hurt me with the words he *didn't* say when passing me by on the other side of the drive without speaking. It was Friday morning now and still there had been no talk between us of any sort, never mind the making up a quarrel sort. I hesitated uncertainly and might even have followed him wherever he was going in order to have it out with him there and then if Henry hadn't appeared from somewhere to stride along by his side. I would be flying off the next day we both knew, yet I deliberately lost myself in an out of the way spot in the gardens after that, in case he might be looking for me later wanting to make up.

It was only as I was actually driving out of the gates on my way home that evening that realisation of just what I was doing finally hit me. Or what I was *not* doing in this case. I wasn't going to be seeing Geoff for two weeks. Supposing something happened to us to keep us away longer. Supposing the unthinkable happened, and there was an accident in which he was killed. How would I ever forgive myself for going off like that with things still the way they were between us?

I am sometimes guilty of leaving things in life to sort themselves out, as they usually do eventually, but on this occasion I didn't really have the option of doing nothing. With no thought to the possible consequences of my actions, I put the car into reverse and, without turning round in my seat, but simply by making use of the mirrors, something I never did in the normal run of things, charged back up the drive, with the engine screaming, heading for where I thought Geoff would be at that moment.

A group of late leaving visitors scattered like the four winds as I went by. Someone coming from the car park, I didn't notice who, stopped their own car in the face of my frenzied approach and then, themselves, went into frantic reverse to escape me, but I wasn't going that far. I spun the car to a halt and left it with engine running and door hanging open, as I raced through the building, crashing door after door behind me as I went.

Geoff was in the last room I came to. Vigorously polishing something as I walked in. He must have heard me coming, but was pretending to be intent on what he was doing. He looked up stony faced as I took the cloth from his hands, flung it dismissively to the floor and oblivious of anyone who might be walking past at that moment, took him in my arms and kissed him fiercely and relentlessly until I could feel the stiffness of his body relaxing, his arms sliding round behind me, and the passion in my kisses returned.

"I love you," I'd barely left myself enough breath to say it.

"I love you too." He breathed, and I realised that the two of us were in tears.

"And I'm sorry," I went on.

"I'm sorry too."

"We're a pair of fools." I said.

"We are, but I think I'm a worse one than you are." He held my face between his hands and kissed my eyes, my nose and my lips.

"I won't argue with that." I said, gasping for breath, when I was able.

"If you don't, it'll be the first time this week that you haven't." He countered.

"Haven't what?" I demanded, as I nibbled at his nose.

"Argued with something I've said." He replied warily.

I held Geoff at arms length and studied him with a worried frown on my face. "Have I been totally unbearable lately?" I wanted to know.

"Very nearly." He answered simply.

"Well, we've no time to talk about it now," I placed a silencing finger on his lips as he seemed about to say more. "I have to go. I'm glad we made it up though and I'll see you in a fortnight and three days."

I drove out of the grounds a few minutes later, much more slowly than I had reversed in, my heart heavier than ever at the prospect of so long a parting now that the pumping adrenalin which had fired me had exhausted its powers. The weekend did pass eventually though, and the Monday, and the Tuesday, and the Wednesday, and...

"Hello. What are you doing here?" Geoff said, as we arrived at the car park at the same moment on the Thursday morning and got out of our cars simultaneously. "I thought you'd be lying out on some beach somewhere now."

And so I would have been, had there not been an air controllers strike in Europe, which had left travellers stranded in airports everywhere. My party amongst them.

"I'm sorry about that," Geoff remarked when I'd completed my explanation.

"Are you?" I asked grimly. "Why?"

"Because I wouldn't dare not to be the way you're looking at me at the moment," he smiled, stepping back out of reach.

"Yes, well," I smiled up into his eyes ruefully, "if you thought I was being totally unbearable before, just be thankful you haven't been with me these past few days." And in my mind, though I couldn't share the thought with him, I made the decision to wean myself off the regular doses of amphetamines which I felt sure, more than the prolonged separation from Geoff, had been the cause of the bad temper and mood swings my companions at the airport had been subjected to during what must have seemed to them to be a very long four days indeed. If I can get hold of some methamphetamines from somewhere, I thought to myself, I'll see what happens if I take them instead.

I'd read you could use them for the occasional binge that would keep you high for several days after you'd taken them, and raise you to heights of sexual performance you could only imagine without them. How useful that was going to be in my relationship with Geoff, now we'd got beyond the sexual highs of those days when we were finally able to get it together, I wasn't sure, but I felt using *any* drugs less regularly than the ones I did now, ought to lessen the long-term effects the ones I was taking might be having on me.".................
....
........"Did you ever manage to give them up? The drugs I mean." I spoke into the break in her story as she paused for breath, getting up from my seat and going over to the fire to stir the embers and put another small log on it.

"What do you think?" She looked across the room at me as I continued what I was doing.

"Probably not. Can anyone *ever* give up drugs that easily once they're hooked on them, even if they want to? Or give up people either?"

"Or give up people either," she smiled, as I went back to the chair and flopped down in it. "Not that I wanted to give up either, if the truth is known. Especially not give up being with Geoff.

I hated Geoff sometimes because he'd forced me out of my cosy environment, and once he'd done that and changed me into what I became because of it, didn't seem to know what to do to satisfy me anymore. Like I said before, I think getting me to fall in love with him had been a dream of his he never really expected to come true and, once he'd achieved that, he simply didn't know what the next step ought to be.

As long as I continued to refuse to leave Jean for him, Geoff was in something of a dilemma, because he was, by nature, someone who preferred to toe the line. He wanted to be my husband, really, not my lover, and didn't settle easily into *that* as a permanent role.

Once he'd forced me out of my own cosy way of life though, I wasn't content just to be the wife of *anyone*. Not Jean, certainly, but not Geoff either, because once *he'd* shaken me up I wanted more than he seemed able to give, and might have left him on more than one occasion, but, because of what we'd been to each other in the beginning, I found I *couldn't* give him up, no matter how he eventually disappointed me, even though I pretended I wanted to."

"Not to yourself, you didn't."

"No, not to myself."

"And your husband?" I probed.

"Jean? I was never addicted to Jean the way I was to Geoff."

"He was addicted to *you* though, wasn't he?"

"Was he?" She looked at me doubtfully. "Why do you say that?"

"He followed you here from France didn't he?" I pointed out. "Because he couldn't bear to be apart from you once you'd returned home."

She smiled as if the idea had never occurred to her before, but pleased her now that I had pointed it out to her. "Yes, I suppose he *did*, now you say it. I'd never thought of it like that before though."

"So he must have had very strong feelings for you." I carried on putting my point across. "And would have taken it badly if he found you preferred some other man to him."

She shook her head firmly at that. "I think," she said doubtfully, "that because you don't know him, you're trying to attribute Jean with feelings and emotions towards me he isn't capable of."

"Perhaps." I said, unconvinced by her protestation.

"*Definitely*." She said it with such conviction I let it lie and went off on a different tack instead.

"So what happened to you in the end?"

"In the *end*?" She looked back at me uncomprehendingly.

"Well you don't work here anymore do you? Haven't had any dealings with Geoff today, despite you both being here." I was afraid I might already know the answer to my question, but wanted to hear from her lips what had happened to them.

"*Is* Geoff here?" She asked a question of her own, avoiding answering either of mine.

"You know he is! You must do!"

"Must I?"

"I would have thought…."

"Yes, you probably would have," she looked me up and down as if she was weighing me up and finding me wanting, "but you're just a boy. Too young to really take in what I've been telling you."

"I don't understand what…" I began, irritated by the dismissive tone of her voice.

"No you don't, do you?" She smiled sadly. "Even now. Never mind. Have another puff of that marijuana and let's see if *that* will make things clearer in your head."

"Marijuana?" I repeated, looking back at her blankly.

"Yes, you know." She said in the tone of voice she might have used if she was explaining it to an idiot, and perhaps she thought she was. "It's another name for cannabis."

"For *what*?"

"God!" Frances sounded almost desperate now at my lack of basic knowledge. "Don't you know *anything*? It's another name for that cigarette you've been enjoying." She shook her head in disbelief. Then, very slowly, with a strange smile on her face, added provocatively, "Go on, have another drag on it."

I took it out of my mouth as hurriedly as if I'd put the lighted end in it by mistake, and examined the glowing tip of it uneasily. It was certainly burning in a strange way, and when I sniffed at it, it had a very strange smell, not at all like a cigarette should. "Have I been smoking cannabis?" I asked uncertainly. Tossing it into the fireplace.

"Of course." She laughed. "What did you think a reefer was?"

"But I don't do drugs." I said indignantly. "I thought you knew that."

"Don't you?" She laughed again. "You seemed to be enjoying *that* one."

"But....." My protest got no further.

"Lighten up Peter," she interrupted sternly, "You're not going to be another Geoff *all* your life are you? I hope not. Now pick that spiff out of the fire, have a good drag on it, and let's not hear another word on the subject."

And she must have had a very persuasive way about her, because the glowing tip of the cigarette I went and retrieved from the fireplace as she'd instructed - in a bid not to be like Geoff Truscott *all* my life, whatever that meant - was the last thing I remember before I woke up late the next morning, slumped in the armchair, in a room grown cold with the dying of the fire and filled with the aroma of that strongly scented cigarette she'd had me smoke before she went.

CHAPTER THIRTEEN

Eddie and Joe had long since gone out to their first jobs of the day when I arrived at work very late that morning. I'd had to go back home after waking up in the rest room the way I had, to put my landlady's mind at rest as to why I didn't come home the previous night. If I hadn't, I was afraid she might get it into her head to report my absence to the police, who would file me as a missing person, or worse, phone my Aunt Maggie to see if I had gone back home to her and forgotten to mention it.

I had been hoping that when I did eventually return to work after doing all this, I would be able to get together with Eddie and hear his account of what he had found out about Frances from his wife, but I had to forsake that notion when I arrived at work to find the bothy devoid of any sign of my fellow workers and, instead, collect up my tools and go off out to work on the hedge again. The unhappy thought occurred to me as I was making my way towards it, that the way I was going on, I might not to be able to keep my job long enough to finish cutting it. So it was that I saw Geoff Truscott again before I saw either of my workmates. Dressed in ordinary clothes now, I was aware of him standing watching me for a long while before I turned the cutters off, expecting him to speak, but he didn't, so I spoke instead. "I don't think Frances is in love with you, you know." I said.

"What?" He blinked, and it was obvious I'd taken him by surprise with *that* opening gambit, so I continued in the theme.

"Things she said about you well…."

"Have you been talking to her?" He interrupted. "Talking to Frances?"

"Yes."

"You had no right to go bothering her." He said heatedly. "No right at all!"

"Of course it might just have been the drugs talking, but…" I began, but was interrupted again.

"Drugs? What are you talking about? Frances doesn't take *drugs*!" He said sharply, and I had the feeling I'd just taken the ground away from beneath the pedestal he'd put her up on.

"She told me she takes crystal meth sometimes," I contradicted evenly, "*and* she had some cannabis with her she got *me* to smoke, so I can promise you she does."

"Where did you meet her?" He demanded. "Not out in the park? I've not seen her there."

"In your rest room," I replied, putting down the hedge cutters once more. "I went there to see if I could find you to ask you something about Frances, and found her instead."

"Well you shouldn't have gone there." He said angrily. "And when you did go there, and found I wasn't around, you should just have gone off without bothering her."

"Made my excuses and left you mean? Like they do in the Sunday papers."

"Something like that." He agreed coldly.

"Well if I had just done that I wouldn't have found out what I did about you would I?" I said with a smile filled with hidden meaning.

"What do you mean by that?" He glared at me furiously. "What did Frances *say* about me?"

"That's for me to know and you to wonder about." I decided to treat him to a little of his own medicine for a while. "Why are you dressed in different clothes now?" I deliberately changed the subject.

"Am I?" He looked down at himself indifferently.

"Last time I saw you, you looked like someone who could have been a Pilgrim Father."

"A Pilgrim *what*?" He said blankly.

"Father. A Pilgrim Father. People who went off to the Americas during the sixteen hundreds because of religious persecution in England." I explained, hoping I'd got the facts, which I wasn't really sure of, right.

"Oh." He sounded none the wiser for my explanation.

"The clothes you're wearing now are almost modern in appearance." I subjected them to further scrutiny.

"Perhaps I'm not wearing a costume, as you call it, anymore." He said, looking down at himself a second time, just as disinterestedly.

"You *are* still Geoff Truscott though?" I persisted.

"Of course." He said, as if there had never been any doubt on *that* score.

"Frances wouldn't say whether or not she *was* Frances." I said a shade irritably at the memory.

"Perhaps it wasn't her." He replied with a sad smile. "Perhaps it was someone else who *does* use drugs."

"She also wouldn't say what happened to any of you at the end." I passed over the challenge in his words that I'd been talking to the wrong person.

"At the end of *what*?" He asked.

"At the end of you and Frances and Jean, her husband." I explained.

"At the end of their *lives* you mean?" He asked in a surprised tone of voice, making me feel as if I had been guilty of extremely bad manners in asking the question.

"Well, no, not at the end of their lives" I said, after a bit of thought about what I had actually been trying to find out from Frances. "How would anyone *know* that, unless their life had had an end? What happened to them after she stopped working here I meant really."

"Do you think that's really the sort of question you should ask anyone?" He said critically. Ignoring the slight back tracking of my answer. "What their end is going to be? Anyway, she wouldn't know. No one is ever told *that*. It would too much for the human mind to cope with."

"But *you* must know what happened to you all." I picked up my broom and gesticulated with it to emphasise my point. "Oh perhaps I should say what is *going to happen* to you all?"

"I know what happened to Frances."

"But not what happened to you?" I wanted to know.

"I know what happened to her husband." Geoff said. "He went back to France."

"But not what happened to you?" I persisted.

"I know what happened to my mother." He went on.

"*But not what happened to you*?" I asked again.

"*My* story is coming to an end." He said with that sad smile of his. "*All* our stories will be coming to an end soon. Yours included eventually. Let me finish telling you mine, and perhaps you'll understand your own better after that."

"Frances said something similar when *she* was saying goodbye to me," I said with a smile of my own, "but I think what is more likely is that I'll be even more confused."

"Perhaps that too," he nodded sagely, "perhaps that too. Can I go on now?"

"If you want to." I made myself comfortable leaning back against the hedge, and waited for him to begin......

...... "You know," he said, smiling his sad smile again, "I had a watch once which had the annoying habit of stopping for no reason and then starting itself again, with the result that, if I didn't happen to glance at it whilst the hands were actually immobile, I could find myself living up to an hour or more behind everyone else. Fine if it prolonged a rest period, or a coffee break, not so good if it delayed my leaving for home. During the months that followed I entertained the notion of searching it out again from the drawer into which I had eventually thrown it in exasperation, to see if, by using it, I could somehow slow time's oncoming rush.

"Time", as Edward Young, a poet and priest who lived during the early seventeen hundreds, was quoted as saying, "flies, death urges, knells call, heaven invites, hell threatens," and though I would never have put it quite so morbidly as that myself, I could certainly see his point. No sooner were the words out of Frances' mouth, than the further restrictions to our being able to spend time together she'd predicted seemed to be upon us, starting with an end to our regular Saturday afternoons together, for reasons I could never quite get to grips with.

"Will you be wanting your dinner early?" My mother continued to enquire every Saturday morning, as she had since I'd started seeing Frances in the afternoons, until, with very bad grace I'm sure, I told her she could serve dinner whenever she chose, unless I told her otherwise.

"Go out with Frances today?" Phil continued to ask whenever we went to the pub for the occasional drink and convivial dissemination of the week's main happenings and I continued to reply that, "No, I didn't anymore."

"You're not seeing her anymore then?" Was his regular follow up question, having apparently digested the information and I would complete the ritual by replying, "Yes, but not on Saturday afternoons."

On Monday evenings we met after work just as we always had done since first we'd started seeing each other, but this seemed to be the only constant factor which remained. Even Thursdays had been obliged to go out of the window because of some sort of family commitments Frances didn't ever really explain to me properly, just saying that they meant she couldn't go out with me on Thursday evenings anymore.

On those Monday evenings when Frances came to my house there were quite frequent chats over cups of tea with my mother, who was getting ever more partial to Frances these days. "She couldn't have been nicer to me if she was my own daughter," she said once, after Frances had brought her a box of her favourite chocolates for no particular reason. She was, nevertheless, still prepared to snipe at our being together whenever opportunity to do so arose.

"I know what it is you do up there," she told me darkly over dinner one day, raising her eyes to the ceiling in order to emphasise the point, but as I had thought that must be fairly obvious by now I let it ride. "I've heard things." That creaking floorboard probably, but there was very little I was able to do about that.

So summer passed and autumn began with most of the old faces at work still watching us disapprovingly, though an intermingling of fresh ones did tend to dissipate the sense of being pariahs from time to time.

"I think you must hold some sort of attraction for Geoff," a new tour guide, filled with the bonhomie of wanting to belong, remarked to Frances when she'd returned to work after a few days off with a cold and we'd gone to the rest room together for coffee in the morning. "Do you know, he hasn't been near the rest room all the time you've been away?" The po faces of his colleagues as he beamed his innocence around the room were a joy to behold.

It was the season of the passing of the autumnal equinox, which men and women of the tribes of ancient Britain used to observe by forming separate circles around which they'd move in opposing directions. The time to pick an apple three days into the waning moon, kiss it and give it to the one whose heart you covet. Hold it and they weaken, eat it and they are yours. Frances had often laughingly accused me of having put a spell on her at the very beginning of things. Now, as the darker, damper evenings drew in, she returned the compliment by putting a worry on me instead.

The cars she and her husband drove had served their purpose, having been bought to raise their profile in the neighbourhood, where a two car family was very unusual, especially with one of the drivers being a woman, but Jean had come to the opinion that they no longer conveyed the image of wealth he had been aiming for, so both had been traded in, sometime back in the spring, as part exchange for new ones. They, like the cars which had preceded them had been, were both Citroens of French origin, for though Jean had spent his life living abroad since he had followed Frances to England, he still wanted to do his bit for the old country by supporting their car industry. Though fully aware that it wasn't really any concern of mine, so long as there was still some means by which Frances could travel to see me, that didn't prevent me from being sorry to see them go.

To me, the little grey Citroen 2cv in which Frances used to drive to our various rendezvous when we first met, had seemed almost as much a part of our being together, as had love itself. There was never any actual courting done in it, it was too small for that, but I became used to looking out for it in discreet corners of the out of the way car parks where she would leave it before transferring to my Triumph Herald. The brand new blue 2cv which replaced it was the latest model, but it would never be anything more than just another car to me. And, though new, the car which she now drove to our rendezvous had both a faulty starter motor and a distressing habit of cutting out as it was going along. Typical of the unreliable nation who had made it, I thought a little unkindly.

It did matter, though, that the car she now had to drive when she went out in the evenings should be such an unreliable one. Illicit activities of any kind, involving, as they do, the need to frequently be in places where you aren't supposed to be, are a hotbed of fears and neuroses. A particular fear of Frances's had always been that her car might not start when she left my house late one night and to be ready for it if this ever happened, I had long ago purchased jump leads and a tow rope, so that at the very least, I would be able to tow her to a point where she was supposed to be, before she phoned anyone to report that she had broken down there.

Another fear, and this was one which had also bothered me whenever we had to leave one of the cars in a lonely spot, was that it might be stolen whilst we were away. The night we came out of my house into a darkened street, devoid, apparently, of Frances's car, was a particularly heart stopping one, until we noticed it tucked in behind a bigger car someone visiting one of my neighbours had parked partly in front of it, obscuring it from view.

The tendency of the engine to cut out was a little more difficult to deal with and, being pressed on the point by me, Frances did eventually confess that it worried her a great deal too. The more so, because her route home from my house took her down some very out of the way lanes, where other traffic was few and far between, and the chance of there being a working public telephone to be found should she require one, remote. The thought of her having to go in search of a cottage with a phone at a time of night when most people in the area had been in bed for hours was daunting to say the least. For that reason I started following her home in my own car, so there would be two of us there to deal with the problem should her car break down at all.............

....

......"Was it worth it?" I broke in on his story.

"Was *what* worth it?" He looked at me a bit blankly. His train of thought broken by my question, it seemed.

"All this subterfuge and stolen moments and the constant fear of being found out. Was it worth it?"

"Of course it was! We wouldn't have carried on seeing each other else would we?"

"I suppose not," I said doubtfully.....................

....

....."We *did* find a different way to go home, though. A much better route, along a main road with more other traffic. That it took a little longer to drive home that way was the only drawback. Frances had always gone the other way because each minute saved on the journey was a minute more to be spent with me. And we were still having trouble with Frances's cars, but not the renegade one this time.

After a lot of prompting from me, Frances had finally bitten the bullet, and reluctantly asked Jean if she could drive the other, more reliable, car, a black Citroen DS, in future, as he didn't have very far to travel from their home to his work. This he had, equally reluctantly, it seemed to me, agreed to let her do, whereupon that car, which until then had always been completely reliable, developed some of the same personality faults the other one had always had once Frances was driving it regularly. On a Saturday, when out of the blue, I was able to answer Phil's question by saying, "Yes, I have seen Frances today," we had one of those afternoons when everything seemed to go wrong, and which ended with

Frances having a tyre burst as she scraped a kerb when being cut up at a roundabout.

The edition of the Guinness Book of Records I consulted later didn't give any times for fastest tyre changes, though it did record a car engine being removed and replaced in forty two seconds by a Royal Marine team of five from Portsmouth. Changing Frances's wheel had taken me longer than that because, as it was a car she hadn't been driving for long, she was unsure where the spare was situated, never mind any of the spanners or levers necessary for replacing the damaged one with it, but I managed it in the end.

"I'm sure something really unpleasant is going to happen to us one day," Frances remarked as I stowed the discarded wheel in the boot. "All these minor mishaps are just practice for the big one, when I get caught with you in my car."

"It was just a puncture, Frances," I tried to put it in proper perspective for her. "The sort of thing that happens to everyone." I was going to add that nothing more threatening was ever likely to happen to us, but, remembering her prediction about us not being able to see each other as often, I held back.

I had once estimated - and I forget the exact figures - that Frances spent a far greater percentage of her time with me than with any other single person. It had been before Hargreaves pulled the reins in on me admittedly, and before her family commitments curtailed our time together still more, but even so.

When Peter Abelard fell in love with his young pupil, Heloise, niece of Canon Fulbert of the cathedral of Paris in twelfth century France, it led him to marriage, a son, and castration at the instigation of the uncle of the bride, who didn't approve of him at all. Abelard had become an abbot, Heloise the head of a new foundation of nuns, and together they had compiled a collection of the love letters they had written to each other when it had all begun. Whilst I hadn't suffered as much as that yet because of my love for Frances, I was beginning to feel that I might just as well have done.

I remembered how, when I had once matched up mine and Frances's birth charts, to see how compatible we were, the angles between our planets had produced some of the strongest ties between two people which it was possible to have. I'd had to laugh though, for the strongest of all were those in opposition to each other. An indication of passion and turbulence as well as of strength.

I was smiling at the thought as I walked across the main lawn of the gardens the following morning on my way to pick up a group of visitors and accompany them to the farm. A woman passing at that moment smiled back and said, "Hello," obviously believing that my smile had been meant for her.

It was a new seasonal tour guide, the latest taken on by Hargreaves to help the rest of us get through the summer. Christine, this one's name was, a very modern woman, who had arrived about a month before and appeared to have a talent for organising everyone and everything, as well as a passion for male tour guides it seemed, because she was constantly inviting Phil and me to her house to look at things which needed doing there and advise her what to do. I don't know if Phil ever took her up on her request for help, but I was constantly declining to go. A variation on coming up to see her etchings if ever I'd heard one, I thought.

Frances had taken great umbrage the moment I'd told her about this. Initially out of fear that I might take the woman up on her offer I suspect, and later because she began to view Christine in much the same light as I had long regarded Phil. It had been quite a pleasant sensation at first to have someone jealous about me, even though, as I had emphatically assured Frances, there was absolutely no reason for her ever to be. Novelty had worn off after a while though and it was unfortunate that Frances should be driving into the car park just as I'd stopped to exchange a word or two with the smiling Christine.

"I suppose that's your way of getting back at me?" Frances blazed when I eventually caught up with her. She had headed off towards the farm area, rather than come into the college and thereby pass us.

"What is?" I asked in all innocence. "And what am I getting at you for anyway?"

"Talking to that...that...Christine! Setting her up for when I'm not around were you? Taking a leaf out of friend Philip's book?"

"Actually I was...." I began to explain bemusedly, but got no further before she cut in.

"Make you feel good does it? Having another string to your bow?"

"Bad night was it?" I asked sympathetically, but that only aggrieved her more.

"Don't humour me! And, no, it isn't that time of month either, before you ask me."

"Well I know that," I pointed out mildly. "I don't take any chances of falling foul of *that*."

"No of course not!" She was stung to still greater flights of eloquence. "The bad temper. The mood swings. *And* I'm getting old. You'd be better off with someone else. Better off with that Christine." She turned on her heel to stalk off.

"Frances! Frances! Wait a moment can't you?" I clutched at her arm to stop her going, missed, there was a ripping sound, and in a moment grand drama had been turned into farce, as I stood looking down at the hood of her jacket, dangling forlornly in my grasp.

"I suppose I could sew it back on for you," I said rather doubtfully when our laughter had finally died away. "As long as you lend me a needle and cotton to do it with that is."

Frances squeezed my hand and carefully took the hood away from me. "I think we've better ways of occupying ourselves than that," she said with a smile. "And still a lot of time in which to do it."

But there wasn't, not for *us* to spend together anyway, because in November Frances fell ill with a flu-like virus, which it seemed impossible for her to shake off. There were a lot of cases of it in the country at the time and doctors seemed as divided about the cure as they were about the cause.

Throughout November and into December it lingered. Sometimes Frances was at work, more often she was not. I found myself frustrated again and again by being completely unable to do anything to help. Or even to go to her house to see how she was.

"We don't see much of Frances these days," my mother remarked shortly before Christmas, as she sat wrapping presents to send to distant relatives.

"No," I sighed, looking up from a book I wasn't really reading.

"Is she still suffering from that virus?" She asked, sorting out a large enough piece of paper for the parcel she was wrapping.

"I'm afraid so." I answered. "She just doesn't seem to be able to shake it off. Seven weeks she's had it now."

"It's worrying." My mother said.

"*Very* worrying," I agreed unhappily.

"And she's always seemed so fit." My mother went on, laying the selected piece of paper out on the table and placing the present into it. "It must be a very nasty thing to get. I hope I don't catch it."

"But, as it happened, she already had." Geoff smiled sadly and went very quiet, as if he was remembering something he would have preferred to forget and I recalled that he'd told me that he knew what had happened to his mother in the end, and now, perhaps, he wished he didn't..
....
......"She didn't get over it then?" I prompted. "Was that when your mother died?"

"No," He smiled that sad smile again. "Not then. There was another death first."

"*Another* death?" I probed.

"Another death." He said heavily, and I realised, with a start, that he was staring down the haunted track as he answered. As if his eyes were being reluctantly drawn towards – what? Something he could see there, but wished he couldn't? With the greatest of trepidation I turned my own eyes towards where his had been looking, but, thankfully perhaps, there was nothing there for me to see.

CHAPTER FOURTEEN

"What did you expect to be there?" Geoff drew my attention back from the haunted track my eyes were still scouring for a sign. "A ghost?"

"I thought there might be something of that sort you keep looking at." I turned back to face him again. Still not sure in my own mind whether I was sorry or sad that there *hadn't* been anything there to see.

"There. And I thought *you* were the one who didn't believe in them." He laughed. "Have I managed to change you views on the subject?"

"Oh I've never had any doubts about the existence of ghosts," I replied irritably. "Just whether or not *you're* one."

"And what's your latest view on that?" He laughed again.

"Still not sure one way or the other."

"I'd better get on with my story then. There isn't much more to tell."

"You mentioned another death." I reminded him.

"Ah yes, I did, didn't I? But not quite yet, because in spring, with Christmas far behind us, the ill health which had plagued us all since the autumn seemed to have dissipated its venom at last. I'd been the last to go down with the virus just into the new year and the first to recover as well. Frances had eventually shaken it off around February, but my mother wasn't completely free of it even then...
....
........She was suffering from a shortness of breath, and a general feeling of weakness which made it so difficult

to get up and down the stairs at home, that she was staying up in her room most days, rather than coming down.

I told Frances and we wondered whether, under the circumstances, we should still go ahead with the day out in the country we'd been planning.

My mother was adamant when I let it slip to her what we had been wondering. "I'll be fine so long as I don't try to move about too much," she assured me. "You go out and enjoy yourselves. You can't disappoint Frances like that."

"I'm not a child to be pacified," was the latter's response when I conveyed the message to her, but we went anyway, and twenty minutes into the outing I began to wonder whether we'd been wise. My companion was obviously unhappy about something. Terse and snappy with me. It crossed my mind that she might have had to lie to someone about what she was going to be doing that day. Frances was never happy about that.

I decided that we should head for a country pub that we'd gone to once before, on the banks of a lake up near Ellesmere. The place didn't have the best of memories for us, but it was close enough to home to be easy to get to for a day out, whilst far enough away for there to be very little chance of us bumping into anyone we knew there. An important consideration in a relationship like ours.

The day was a sunny one, and pleasantly warm, and if Frances was hardly speaking to me, at least she was there. I decided to make the best of it I could and not respond to her terseness in any way. Instead, I concentrated on finding the way to the pub where we were going to be eating that day, forgetting in the excitement of being out with Frances at last, what we'd discovered about the pub when we'd been there before. That, though it had great character, with half timbering and massive beams across the fireplace and the ceilings, it also, unfortunately, had service which was distressingly slow.

We had seen the two coaches out in the car park when we arrived there and hesitated at first to go in. It was the only pub I knew of in the immediate vicinity, however, and I was feeling by then that a rest from being cooped up in the car together might be even better than a change. As luck would have it there was a table by a window just being vacated as we pushed our way in through the crowd, so we placed our order with the hot and harassed waitress, who was having to deal with everyone on her own, and sat uncomfortably, making desultory conversation from time to time.

Difficult enough to stay civil anyway under those circumstances, amongst that hubbub of chattering charabancers. We could have well done without the elderly lady who came to claim the two spare seats at our table for herself and a friend, who was apparently stranded at the bar. It was too much like the breaks at Moorecroft House had originally been when we were both first working there and our workmates were intent on preventing us enjoying a tete-a-tete.

She must have taken the silence between us, which by then you could have cut with a knife, as being in some way attributable to her presence because, after looking around the room several times with increasing desperation, she leaned forward and announced in a conspiratorial whisper, "I've just noticed a free table in the corner, so I think I'll go and keep that for my friend instead. I can see when two people want to be alone. I was young once myself you know."

"So was I." Frances muttered for my ears alone and suddenly we were smiling again. Her hand found mine under the table and we were planning what to do with the remainder of the afternoon.

"That place I took you to the first time we came to this pub isn't so very far away from here," I said thoughtfully.

"What!" She exclaimed. "That dreadful woodland you had me staggering through after I'd dressed up for the occasion?"

"Well I didn't know that you were going to turn up looking like a refugee from a royal garden party did I?" I retorted. "Otherwise, I would have taken you to Buckingham Palace instead."

"And I didn't know *you* well enough then to know that when you take a girl out to show her a good time she needs wellington boots and overalls." She smiled at the memory.

"Do you remember how you told me that our relationship had to end there and then?" I said, smiling myself at the memory of our foolishness in thinking it. "That it didn't have any future?"

"I could have saved us both a lot of grief if I'd stood by that, couldn't I?" She smiled at that memory too, but her smile had changed to a sad one.

"Could have robbed us of a lot of pleasure too." I responded sharply, hurt by the suggestion.

"Perhaps." She refused to give way.

"Perhaps?" I could see the waitress making her gradual way towards us with a plate in either hand. "Now you don't really mean that do you?"

"The trouble is, Geoff, that I do." She used a paper napkin to mop up the pool of gravy splashed on the table when her meal was rather heavily put down in front of her. "With increasing frequency the longer this affair of ours goes on."

I picked up my knife and fork and reflected on the moody silence which had come down between us again. It hadn't been like that when we'd been this way before I remembered.

Then it had been autumn and Frances saw our new love as an adventure, now in spring a year and a half later, she was suggesting it was sometimes an encumbrance. We finished our food and then drove the quarter of a mile to the woodland we had spoken about, parked, and walked hand in hand down a lane bordered on either side by hazel bushes hung with catkins.

"This is where I first decided I wanted to study the lute for my Royal Academy of Music degree." We had stopped to look through a fringe of trees towards a meadow, where horses grazed beside a fast flowing stream, on the other side of which banks of flowering blackthorn bushes rose above each other up the side of a hill. "Because of an old man I came across when I was walking beside the river here one day. He was sitting on the bank over there and playing a lute for all he was worth, and I felt as soon as I saw him there, as if I was drawn to playing the instrument myself for some reason.

When I spoke to the man, he said he was playing outdoors like that, because his family wouldn't let him practice indoors. I thought to myself, I live on my own, so no one would be able to object to *my* playing. I was enchanted by the sound of the music he was playing.

Did you know that traditionally, lutes are made from a lot of different woods? Yew wood, that you get from trees like those growing over there, was the most common wood for making the ribs and the back of the lute. It's easier to bend than sycamore, the other wood people used to use for making them, and being a dark wood, doesn't need as much skill when varnishing things made with it.

Sycamore was better used for the neck of a lute, because it's strong and stable and not so inclined to warp. Spruce is favourite for the sound board. Did I tell you that the last time we came this way?" I smiled at the memory of the occasion.

"You did." She steadfastly refused to return my smile.

So now I was boring, as well as an encumbrance! We walked on past a notice warning that fishing was prohibited and I had another try.

"I want to take a photograph of you." I took out the little folding box camera I never usually remembered to bring with me.

"Whatever for? I don't like the look of myself in photographs at all."

"You won't be seeing them, will you? *I* will. And I need something to moon over and remind me of what you look like during those really long separations we have these days." I burst into a quick rendition of 'If I had a talking picture of you'.

"I should think you'd do better to forget," but she posed sitting on a stile where I had placed her, and then leaning up against a signpost indicating a footpath to somewhere or other, and then, "No. That's enough!" So I had to be content.

It was pleasant down there by the river. We'd walked across a cornfield, where the lush green growth of young wheat still hugged the ground, down another lane, over a narrow bridge, and then along a soil track adjacent to some watercress beds. There we went away from the path we were following, into a clearing hidden from the outside world by a fringe of bushes. We sat against the trunk of a young beech tree and, after a while, Frances tickled my nose with a blade of grass, as I lay looking up at the sky. I reached up and drew her down towards me, to smother her with kisses.

She resisted at first, as she generally did those days, then seemed to come to some sort of decision within herself, because she looked down at me so - I don't know – so *sadly*, as she allowed me to slip the loose dress she was wearing up over her head and helped me to ease her out of the little she was wearing under it. It had been a long time since we'd last made love I remember, but there, away from the prying eyes which always seemed intent on watching our every move when we were at Moorecroft House, we made love again, with all the fire and passion of our earlier days together. Almost as if…." His voice tailed off and I looked at him sharply….

…….."Almost as if?" I prompted.

"Almost as if she knew it would never happen again," Geoff said sadly. "I loved her then as I would have loved her if life had only allowed us to make love like that when we had only just met. Before time robbed our passion of its freshness. Before reality took *its* toll too. Eventually, though, we drew apart from each other and lay there side by side without speaking, just enjoying each other's company, before coming back together and, though I hadn't thought it possible, making love a second, even more passionate, time.

"Happier now?" I asked, when, after an unbelievable *third* time of making love with Frances, we eventually made our way back through the woods, and across the field, to my car. "Happier than you were I mean?"

"I'm sorry about that." Frances squeezed my hand apologetically. "I don't really know what it was all about myself. Just a mood of some sort I suppose. I felt …….. I don't know......Something**....................................**

........."Fey probably," Geoff said thoughtfully, and I realised with a start that he was looking at me, talking to *me* again, not relating past times, "because that was the last day we ever shared together before….before….." He blinked away a tear or two, and turned his head away from me as he stared off into the distance, but said no more. Looking down the haunted track again, as if, this time, he was going hurry off along it. Towards something? Towards a future with Frances? Away from something? Away from me? Away from the past? Away from memories he could bear no more? Towards or away from what, I was never to know.

I stared at him uncomprehendingly as he turned his head back towards me again, returning my stare, but saying no more. The story of his and Frances' love affair having apparently come to an end. "You can't just stop *there*!" I said fiercely, as he continued to stand silently, but looking away into the distance again now. "You *have* to tell me the rest of the story now you've taken it that far. *Why* was it the last time you had together? *Why* didn't you ever get together again? What happened to her? She can't have just disappeared. *I've* seen her, even if you haven't! In the rest room last night."

I rattled on, but still he made no response. Just stood there staring into apparent nothingness, as if he had suddenly been struck by something, but by what? By that forbidden knowledge that had been hidden from him until then? The knowledge that no one is supposed to be privy to, for fear its possession brings about the total destruction of their minds. The exact time and circumstances of what his own death was going to be? If he *was* dead. And I still wasn't certain of *that*. Or that he wasn't just a strange man having a private joke at my expense. Or even that he wasn't part of a joke my new workmates were having with me for some reason.

"Peter!" A voice I didn't recognise called my name from somewhere in the distance. A woman's voice? A man's voice? I couldn't be sure even when it called again, "Peter!" With more urgency the second time.

"Go away!" I mouthed the words without saying them out loud. Continuing to stare uncomprehendingly at Geoff Truscott, who remained stubbornly silent. "Go away!" I breathed again, when the voice called my name a second and then a third time.

"I can't come!" I turned briefly in the direction the unknown voice was calling to me from, to call back, out loud this time. In response, if it was a response, there came a sound like wind whispering through long grass, which disappeared into the far distance down the haunted track away from me with a sigh. Was it Geoff Truscott leaving my side? I don't know. All I can say for certain is that when I turned back to where he had been, he was no longer there.

No one came as a result of the voice calling and in the end I collected up my tools for the last time and made my way slowly back along the haunted track with them, staggering all the way back to the yard like a man carrying an unsupportable weight on his shoulders.

"Why were you calling me?" I asked Joe, who was the only person in sight when I got there.

"*Was* someone calling you?" he answered question with question, looking up from cleaning a fork and a spade in the water trough in the corner by the bothy. "Wasn't me if there was."

"Must have been Eddie then. *Someone* was calling me." I insisted, taking the tools out of my barrow and laying them on the ground. Ready for me to wash and dry when he'd finished with the trough.

"Well if he *was*, I didn't hear him." Joe got on with what he was doing. "What do you think he wanted you for? Whoever it was who was calling you. If it was a 'he,' that is?"

"I don't really know." I shook my head doubtfully. "I thought it was a bloke when I first heard it, but now I'm not so sure. If it wasn't either of *you*, who could it have been?"

"Frances – what did you call her – Delamore?" He said with a funny sort of smile. "Not likely to have been her though is it? Not after what Eddie found out about her last night."

"Eddie found out something about Frances Delamore last night?" I said excitedly. "What did he find out?"

"You'd better ask Eddie that." Joe replied easily. "I wouldn't do it now though." He advised.

"Why not?" I didn't like the sound of that. I needed Eddie to be on my side at the moment. Not for me to be in his bad books.

"You're not exactly his favourite person right now." He explained.

"Why not?" I asked again.

"He's had a complaint from Montgomery about you leaving the tour guide's rest room in a bit of a state. Says you broke in yesterday and spent most of the night in there. Knows it was you, because you left your bag behind. Stuffed full of funny baccy it was."

"That wasn't *me*!" I said indignantly.

"Who was it then?" He asked disbelievingly.

"Frances."

"Frances Delamore? The tour guide who….." He laughed. "Well I'd come up with a better story than *that* if I was you. If you want to keep your job here that is. *Do* you want to keep your job here?"

"Of course I do!" I said indignantly.

"Well, if you take *my* advice, just keep shtum, and don't say anything but sorry when Eddie's laying into you. And whatever you do, don't try to put the blame on Frances Delamore."

"Why not?" I glared at him. "I know I went into their room uninvited – I didn't *break* into it though - and

I didn't do any damage to it whilst I was in there. And anything smoked in there belonged to Frances. It was me who smoked it admittedly, whatever it was, but it was her who had taken it there and *wanted* me to smoke it."

"Well….." he shrugged. "Oops, here we go. I'm off. I've done my bit. Now you'll have to sort things out on your own." He shot out past the advancing Eddie, and in a moment I was standing on my own, facing a fire-breathing foreman who knew something I didn't know about the tour guides I had been dealing with for the past two days.

CHAPTER FIFTEEN

Eddie Ponting sighed and stood looking at me with his hands on his hips. "I don't know what to make of you young Peter, really I don't. With all these stories you've been telling us about the ghosts you've been talking to since you started working in the gardens. What Mr Montgomery here is going to make of it I don't know." He nodded his head towards the tall thin man, with a shock of grey hair, who was standing behind him. "I know Joe and me made a bit of a joke about it in the beginning, putting ideas into your head, so perhaps we're partly to blame for what's happened since, but enough is enough. There is *no* ghost at Moorecroft House."

"Not even a Grey Lady?" I said disappointedly.

"Especially not a Grey Lady. Isn't that right Mr Montgomery?"

"It is," The other man replied gravely in a deep voice. "Read the guide book and it will tell you so."

"I couldn't get hold of one last night when I went looking."

"Pity" Eddie went on, "because if you *had* you might have noticed that it never mentions her at all. There's no more truth in *her* haunting the place than there is in Anne Boleyn haunting it. They made the story up when they started running ghost walks here. That's the case with most ghosts you'll find. None of them have any real existence, I'm afraid. They're all just figments of somebody's imagination. Isn't that true Mr Montgomery?" He half turned towards the man behind him.

"It is." He replied in that voice reminiscent of Valentine Dyall.

"*None* of them?" I looked at him, not wanting to believe what I was being told.

"*None* of them." Eddie glared at me as if I was disputing what he was saying to me, rather than, as was really the case, confirming it reluctantly. According to the Guinness Book of Records, the most haunted village in England is Pluckley in Kent, where, is says in the guide book," he put on a posh voice and spoke as if reading from it, "visitors may encounter a highwayman, a green man, a miller and a dog amongst the ghosts which frequent it." Then, reverting to his normal tones, "And if you can find me anyone who actually *has* encountered any of them, I'll give you twenty quid.

Tulloch Castle Hotel, at Dingwall in Ross and Cromarty, tells people in its brochures that it has a ghost which rattles door handles, and a green lady, who is the ghost of someone who died falling down a spiral staircase, but that's just to draw the punters in.

Like it is at Ruthin Castle, Ruthin, Denbighshire, which is supposed to have a grey lady of its own, who is the ghost of a woman who killed her lover with an axe. Has anyone ever seen her though? I think not."

"What about Raynham Hall in Norfolk, where someone took a photo of a Brown Lady, they said was the ghost of Lady Dorothy Townsend, wife of Turnip Townsend, who appeared on the stairs. I've seen *that* photo, so she must have existed." I raised an objection to his rampant demolition of every ghost there had ever been in the country.

"Never appeared again though, has she, since that photo was taken in the 1930s." He rode roughshod over my defence of all things ghostly. "And not likely to either, in my opinion.

Gwydir Castle in the Conwy Valley now, that has a north wing which is said to be haunted by the ghost of a servant girl murdered after becoming pregnant. It also has a phantom dog and crying children.

The Talbot Hotel, Oundle, has a staircase which was once part of Fotheringay Castle, and which Mary Queen of Scots is said to haunt by re-enacting her walk down those stairs to her execution. Just like the Grey Lady here is supposed to re-enact events surrounding *her* execution, and we all know how *that* story came about!"

"My Aunt Maggie takes herself off to see a medium every Thursday. And *she* believes she has contact with spirits there, whatever you say." I decided it was time to strike a blow in defence of my family's beliefs and risk annoying Eddie further, whatever Joe had warned me my best course of action would be.

"Does she now?" Eddie looked at me a bit old fashioned as he said it. "Well, if we'd known you were susceptible to such things as ghosts, ghouls, and things that go bump in the night, because of the way you'd been brought up, we wouldn't have made a joke about the haunted track when we set you working there."

"Because I'm gullible, you mean?" I caught the inference in his words.

"Susceptible I said, and susceptible I meant." He contradicted me. "I didn't say that your aunt's beliefs are *wrong*, just that I wouldn't have set you working where I did if I'd known about them before.

Or in the garden of what's reputed to be the most haunted house in England. A mansion on the outskirts of Beccles in Suffolk, called Roos Hall, which has a hanging tree in its grounds - an oak tree once used as a gibbet, where many a local criminal ended his days.

Careston Castle at Angus is supposed have a hanging man too. The shade of a man hung for stealing a branch from the laird's favourite tree is sometimes seen dangling from trees in the neighbourhood. Especially by folk on their way back from the pub after having a few too many, I shouldn't wonder.

At Fordill in Fife, a man whose master killed two soldiers at the village mill and then fled to escape the consequences, was hung in his place, and is now sometimes to be seen hanging from trees in the neighbourhood, with his eyes bulging from their sockets. And at Grindleford in Derbyshire, the ghost of a man who tried unsuccessfully several times to hang himself on trees at Stoke Hall, in the village, and then hung himself successfully from a beam in a barn, when the branches of the trees kept breaking under his weight, can be seen running around the trees searching for a suitable one again."

"Only by people on their way home from the local pub after having a few too many bevvys in your opinion, though!" I cut in, thinking of my Grandfather, and my Aunt Maggie, and unable to keep quiet anymore.

"Most of them, I reckon," Eddie glared at me for my interruption, then continued. "One of the most haunted buildings in Wales is said to be The Skirrid Inn at Llanfihange, which has a beam on the staircase which once served as a gibbet. Over 180 people, some of whom are said to haunt the place, have been hanged on that over the years. You notice a common theme here Peter?" He interrupted himself.

"The most haunted house on the National Trusts' list of their properties in Britain is Blickling Hall in Norfolk, which has a list of ghosts a mile long. Including the very busy Ann Boleyn, of course, her brother George, and Sir John Fastolfe among the phantoms who are supposed to put in an appearance *there.*

Not on the same day as Anne is haunting here, of course, or the Tower of London, where she has the company of Henry IV, Thomas Beckett and the Countess of Salisbury, whose ghost is pursued and hacked to death by the ghost of the axe man who gave chase when she fled from the scaffold.

Of course, Anne and her family didn't have their deaths foretold by trees in the grounds of the houses they owned, but some people do. A lime tree in the grounds of Cuckfield Park, at Cuckfield in Sussex, drops a branch whenever a member of the family in the nearby house dies, and a farm at Stalybridge, in Lancashire, is home to a tree with leaves which are said to shake violently just before the death of any member of the family who lives there, regardless of wind or weather conditions.

It probably isn't a yew tree like those that make up the hedges you've been cutting since you got here, because they don't have the type of leaves to shake like that, but they *do* often have the reputation of being haunted in some way, simply because of their appearance of great antiquity, even when they're not really that old. The yew grove at Cholderton in Wiltshire probably *is* very old, because it was sacred to the druids in days gone by, and the rites they once carried out there, under the canopy of the trees, left the grove with a sad and oppressive atmosphere if you venture into it, according to people who are susceptible to those things......."

"People like me you mean?" I wanted to say, but didn't, as he went on.

"....Just as the second yew tree on the right after entering the church yard at Nevern in Dyfed affects some people who go near it. It's known as the bleeding yew, because blood is said to constantly drip from the stump where a branch was once severed.

Brockdish Hall, near Harleston in Norfolk, now. That's said to be haunted by a ghost with a connection to another of the druid's sacred plants. Mistletoe. The Mistletoe Bride, the ghost is called, and it's supposed to be the spirit of a girl who was playing hide and seek with her husband on their wedding night, and hid herself in a chest which could only be opened from the outside. Unfortunately for her, no one was able to find her that night, and no one looked in the chest to see if that was where she was when she went missing. Though you would have thought her husband, driven by the sort of urges a bridegroom usually has towards his bride on his wedding night, would have thought of looking in there just in case. The riddle of her disappearance wasn't solved until fifty years later, when the chest was opened, and a skeleton wearing a bridal gown was found clasping a sprig of mistletoe.

Harleston is somewhere I know quite well. I often used to stay there with my grandmother when I was a child. Down one of the lanes there was a big old house

167

with a boarded up window in the upper storey, behind which was a bedroom the owners wouldn't use because it was said to be so badly haunted. I believed in ghosts when I was a lad, just like you do now, before experience showed me there were no such things, and was fascinated by that house and its boarded up window. I used to stand looking at it for hours whenever I was staying in the village, hoping that the ghost would put in an appearance, but it never did.

Nor did the ghost of one of the Bishops of London, who was supposed to come up behind unwary gardeners working at Fulham Palace and tap them on the shoulder if they weren't working hard enough. Of course, that might have been because when I was there I was never idle enough to draw his attention." He stopped his discourse and smiled at me in a far friendlier fashion that I had expected after Joe's warning about the state of his temper. "You're looking at me a bit old fashioned, young Peter. Not liking having your ghosts, ghoulies and things that go bump in the night put into perspective eh?"

"Ones like Frances Delamore, you mean?" I ignored Joe's friendly warning to avoid the subject like the plague and mind my ps and qs and went straight for the jugular.

"Hmm," he frowned and the bonhomie went out of his voice. "You do like to live dangerously don't you boy?" He said evenly. "All right, you have it your way. Let's talk about Frances Delamore and – what was the fellow's name?"

"Geoff Truscott." I supplied.

"Geoff Truscott, right. Let's talk about them and what I've found out about them since you started asking me about them, and then, perhaps, you can explain to me how you could have spent the days since you got here talking to two people who have been dead a long time. A *very* long time."

"*Dead*?" I cut in quickly. So Geoff Truscott *had* been a ghost. And Frances too I suddenly realised. Both of them dead a very long time according to Eddie. Despite me speaking to her only yesterday, and Geoff just hours ago. "Are you sure?" Somehow I didn't want that to be the case.

Eddie was looking at me in a far more kindly manner that I had expected. "I'm afraid so Peter," he said gently, "there's no doubt on *that* score. It's all here in these newspaper cuttings which Mr Montgomery kindly sorted out of his archive in the attic for us. Why don't you read through them now and see if that settles in your mind why you *can't* have been talking to any of the people involved since you got here?"

He handed me a small file, with the newspaper cuttings in it set behind plastic covers. "Take them in there and read them," he indicated the bothy, "and Mr Montgomery and me will be coming in to join you in a while to accept any apologies you might like to be making to either of us."

With a heavy heart, and a sense of great disappointment, I took the file he was holding out to me, and went into the bothy with it, clearing a space on the table to spread things out on, then sat down and began to read a sequence of newspaper cuttings containing accounts mostly of events which had happened in the locality in

1962. Just one undated cutting, which wasn't behind a cover, but clipped loosely into the file, seeming to be more recent.

....

The little hamlet of Carbury, in Shropshire, was rocked yesterday by a double murder involving two of its most illustrious residents. Jean Delamore, heir to the Delamore hotel dynasty of Grenoble in France, and his wife, Frances, who worked as a tour guide at nearby Moorecroft House.

At first it was speculated that the deaths might have resulted from the murder of Frances Delamore by her husband, who then committed suicide, after he discovered that she was having an affair with another of the tour guides at Moorecroft House. Further investigations on the part of the police, however, now seem to point to a double murder, perhaps as the result of a burglary that went wrong. Although the couple lived a relatively low key life in this country, Monsieur Delamore was a very wealthy man in his own right, and was in line to one day inherit the Delamore millions from his father, who still runs the family business in France. In France, the curtains were drawn at the Delamore mansion and no one from the family was available for comment. We will keep you informed of any further developments as they occur.

....

Police in Shrewsbury say there is no truth in the rumour that they have received information from a secret source which will lead to an arrest soon in the case of the Delamore double murder at nearby Carbury last week, which the popular press has dubbed the House of

Horror Murders, because of the amount of blood shed by the victims.

The bodies of the two victims were found slumped across each other in one of the bedrooms of the house, Monsieur Delamore fully clothed, his wife naked. Both had been killed by repeated blows to the head with a blunt instrument of some sort, which had left the two unfortunates lying in a veritable lake of their own blood.

....

Police refuse to confirm or deny whether or not they have arrested someone for the House of Horror Double Murders at Carbury, in Shropshire.

....

Police refuse to confirm or deny whether the man arrested for the double murder of Monsieur and Madame Delamore at Carbury, in Shropshire, is Geoffrey Truscott, another of the tour guides at nearby Moorecroft House, where Madame Delamore worked, and the man informed sources there say she had been having an affair with for more than a year.

....

Police have charged Geoffrey Truscott of 16 Hampden Road, Shrewsbury with the double murder of Monsieur and Madame Delamore of Carbury, also in Shropshire.

....

The centre court at Shrewsbury was packed today when the trial of Geoffrey Truscott, of 16 Hampden Road, Shrewsbury, charged with murdering his former lover, Frances Delamore and her husband, Jean, began.

The court was told how Madame Delamore had been lured into an affair with Truscott entirely against her wishes and how he had put pressure on her in many ways to make her continue the affair long after she wished it to end.

The accused sat stony-faced as evidence was presented of how he had forced his victim to take a drug called methamphetamine, sometimes known as meth, speed, or crystal, which can be smoked, inhaled or swallowed, and is a powerful stimulant of the nervous system, which would give her the increased sexual desire and stamina necessary to satisfy his cravings, but had turned her into an addict who had to have drugs in order to be able to carry on with her ordinary life. The drugs hadn't had time to kill her before Truscott had done it in another way, but would have destroyed her nerve cells and nerve connections if used for too long. In the end, however, even all that Madame Delamore had given up, or changed in her life because of Truscott, hadn't been enough and he had threatened that if she didn't leave her husband and go off with him, he was going to kill him.

Evidence was brought by the police to show that what had actually happened had been that Madame Delamore had given in to Truscott's threats and demands and was actually in bed with him in the marital home when her husband returned unexpectedly halfway through the day and surprised them there together. Enraged by his discovery, he had seized a hammer, which he had been using for some DIY at the house the previous day, and attacked Truscott with it. A fight had ensued, during which Truscott, under the influence of the methamphetamine he also habitually took to stimulate him during sex sessions with his lover, and which had the other side effect of lessening the inhibitions of regu-

172

lar users, and altering their self control when faced with any degree of opposition, wrestled the hammer from the angry husband and laid into him, beating him about the head with it. When Madame Delamore then tried to intervene on the side of her husband, Truscott struck her in her turn with such fierce blows to her head with the hammer, that she too collapsed to the ground in a pool of her own blood. Horrified at what he had done when he came to his senses, her assailant then fled the scene, but the hammer, still covered in the victim's blood, was subsequently discovered in his locker at work, as the result of an anonymous tip-off to the police, along with his own supply of the methamphetamine he had forced Madame Delamore to take. Obviously overwhelmed by the enormity of what he had done the accused, known to be a loner with few friends and an ungovernable temper, had made no attempt to flee to escape punishment for his crime, but was found in bed asleep, still apparently under the influence of the methamphetamine, when police broke down his front door and forced their way in hours later.

Geoffrey Truscott admitted that he had had a relationship with Madame Delamore, but disputed that it was an affair in the sense the court meant, or that he had ever threatened to kill Monsieur Delamore, for whom he had never felt any animosity at all. He denied he was in any way to blame for the murder of either victim, that he had forced Madame Delamore to take any form of drug for whatever reason, that he was under the influence of drugs himself at any time in the proceedings, or that he had ever taken drugs at all. He seemed resigned to what was happening to him, and offered no defence to back up his bald statement that he was not guilty of the crimes he was accused of.

....

Geoffrey Truscott, of 16 Hampden Road, Shrewsbury, has been found guilty of the double murder of Monsieur and Madame Delamore of Carbury, in Shropshire, and was remanded for sentencing next week.

....

The death occurred today at 16 Hampden Road, Shrewsbury, of Mrs Emily Truscott, mother of Geoffrey Truscott, recently found guilty at Shrewsbury Crown Court, of the House of Horror Hammer Murders of Monsieur and Madame Delamore of Carbury. Neighbours at Hampden Road said that Mrs Truscott had been ailing for some time, and that her son being found guilty of charges she believed to be unfounded, seemed to have hastened her death.

....

Geoffrey Truscott, found guilty of the double murder of Monsieur and Madame Delamore of Carbury, in Shropshire, has been sentenced to death for the murders and will be taken to a place of execution to pay for his crimes on a date and at a time yet to be arranged. His lawyer, Miss Madeleine McIver of McIver and Gibbons, solicitors of Shrewsbury, says he is resigned to his fate and will not be appealing.

The death of Madame Delamore, followed by that of Mr Truscott's mother so shortly afterwards, probably as a direct result of him being found guilty of a crime he didn't commit, had robbed Mr Truscott's life of all purpose and any need to go on. Miss McIver said on his behalf.

174

....

The body of Jean Delamore, one of the victims of the House of Horror Hammer Murders perpetrated in Carbury, in Shropshire, in June, for which Geoffrey Truscott was recently found guilty and sentenced to death at Shrewsbury Crown Court, has been flown back to Grenoble in France for burial in the family mausoleum there. the Delamore family has asked the press to leave them to mourn his passing in private.

A spokeswoman for McIver and Gibbons, solicitors of Shrewsbury, who represented Geoffrey Truscott when he was tried for, and found guilty of, the murder of Frances Delamore and her husband Jean at Carbury, in Shropshire, has refused to confirm or deny reports that the burial of Frances Delamore recently, at a secret location near Shrewsbury, was paid for out of the estate of Mrs Emily Truscott, who died during her son's trial, or that the rest of her estate will be going to various charities. Geoffrey Truscott, her only surviving relative at the time of her death, is shortly to be executed for the two murders.

....

Geoffrey Truscott, the House of Horror Hammer Murderer, was executed at Shrewsbury Prison at 10 am this morning, for the double murders of Monsieur and Madame Delamore of Carbury, in Shropshire, earlier in the year. Right up until his death the prisoner maintained that he was innocent of any crime, except that of falling in love with a married woman, but said that once someone else had robbed him of Frances Delamore, his life no longer had any purpose to it, and he had no wish to go on living in a world in which she didn't exist.

······························

*The house in Carbury in Shropshire, where the hor-
rific murders of Monsieur and Madame Delamore,
which the popular press dubbed the House of Horror
Hammer Murders, were carried out, has been demol-
ished on the wishes of the Delamore family. A spokes-
man for the Delamore hotel dynasty of Grenoble in
France, whose son Jean was one of the victims, said that
they didn't want the house to become a place of macabre
pilgrimage. A small park has been laid out where the
house stood, for the benefit of the community of Carbury.*

······························

*Authorities at Shrewsbury Prison, have refused to
confirm or deny rumours circulating locally, that the
bodies of prisoners executed at the gaol between 1902
and 1962, eight in number, all men, including that of the
notorious House of Horror Hammer Double Murderer,
Geoffrey Truscott, who was the last prisoner executed
there thirty years ago, in November 1962, have been exhumed from the unmarked graves in which they were
buried, cremated at a local crematorium, and the ashes
scattered in a local park.*

······························

I looked up from the last of the newspaper cuttings
when I had read them, feeling a sudden sympathy for
Geoffrey Truscott, who I was sure wasn't guilty of the
crimes for which he had been executed. How terrible it
must have been for him sitting there in court whilst his
lover's betrayal of him and his dreams had been laid bare
to the world. And to go down in history as the House of

Horror Hammer Murderer! How terrible that must have been for such a gentle man. I had intended to speak to Eddie Ponting and ask if it had been in the grounds of Moorecroft House that the prisoners' ashes had been scattered, but he wasn't there for some reason, so, instead, I had to address myself to Mr Montgomery, who *was*. "There are two things wrong with this you know?"

"What" he replied sarcastically, "Besides the two people he murdered?"

"No, the suggestion that Geoff Truscott started Frances off on drugs, and the suggestion that he would force her to leave her husband.

I've talked to both of them since I've been here and Geoff didn't even know that Frances was *taking* drugs, let alone start her off on them. And he *wasn't* pressuring her to leave her husband, because he truly *did* believe that they were destined for each other and that things would eventually turn in his favour. In any case, he was too gentle a man to have ever have done anything as violent as that. I can believe that he just gave up and didn't offer any defence when he realised that Frances had betrayed him with someone else, and that someone else had killed her and her husband, though."

"Wait a minute, wait a minute," my companion said quickly, obviously startled by my assertion. "Not so fast. Go back a bit. You say you talked to both of them?"

"Yes." I replied defiantly, sensing his overwhelming disbelief.

"Son," he ran his hands through his hair, leaving it pushed up into wild turrets, and it was apparent from the look on his face that he set no value at all in what I was saying, "you've *imagined* you talked to both of since you've been here, that's all. They're both dead. Have been for years. So you *can't* have spoken to them. And even if you had, and you were right, it would be too late to do anything for either of them now."

"Why did they appear to me then?" I demanded. "If it's too late to do anything for them now?"

"What?" Montgomery looked more than a bit bemused by my words, and I couldn't really blame him for that.

"Why did they both appear to me yesterday and today?" I repeated the question. "They've never appeared to anyone before have they?"

"Not that I know of, no." He shook his head emphatically.

"So why now? Why the sudden urgency? What's changed? What happened to upset Geoff's equilibrium?"

My companion shook his head sadly. "Listening to you Peter, I'd have to say that if *anyone* has an upset equilibrium in all of this, it's you. I mean, listen to yourself! Geoffrey Truscott was tried and found guilty of a particularly nasty crime a lot of years ago! That's the nub of it. Anything else is just your imagination at play."

I shook my head fiercely, then suddenly remembered the last of the newspaper cuttings. "Do you think it's because Geoff's body has been exhumed and cremated and his ashes scattered somewhere? Do you think they might have been scattered in *this* park?"

"This isn't a park Peter." He pointed out gently. "And I think I would have known if someone had been scattering Geoffrey Truscott's ashes here. Perhaps the reason no one has ever seen him here before is simply that there's never been anyone work here before who was daft enough to *think* they saw him."

"You don't believe me then, when I tell you I've spoken to both of them since I've been working here?" I asked, knowing only too well what the answer to *that* question was going to be.

"In a nutshell Peter, no." He said firmly. Supplying me with what I had expected.

"But what about the evidence? The evidence I know is wrong. Who gave it to the police?" I tried a different tack.

"I don't think it says where they got their information from in any of the reports, does it?" My companion said after having a think about it.

"No." I agreed. "But whoever it was might have had a motive of their own."

"*What* motive?" He asked in tones of disbelief.

"The motive of covering up the murder *they* did!" I replied fiercely. "After all, if Geoff *didn't* do it, then someone else must have. The police didn't have forensic science to help them in those days like we do now. No way to check something like the murder weapon for DNA like they do in those cold case programmes they show on tv."

"But there wasn't anyone else involved, except Truscott. He was the only suspect. The police didn't need to go looking for anyone else." Mr Montgomery objected.

"What about Phil?" The idea suddenly hit me over the head like a sledgehammer.

"Phil?" Mr Montgomery repeated blankly.

"Geoff's friend Phil." I explained. "He tried it on with every woman he ever came in contact with, including Frances. He might have tried his luck with her one last time, and things got out of hand."

"Surely that would have come out at the time?" My companion said dismissively.

"How?" I knocked the ball firmly back into his court. "There was no one there to take Geoff's side in it all, apart from Phil. And if he was protecting his *own* back, covering his *own* tracks! Well!" A sudden thought struck me. "What became of him?"

"I don't know." Montgomery shook his head, but I could see that I had won my point and that my ideas were taking root with him now. "That was well before my time."

"You must have *something* about him in your records somewhere though." I pushed home my advantage. "Where he went to, perhaps."

"You know, there are still some old files around from those days." He said thoughtfully. "Shall we go and have a look at them? See what we can turn up?"

"Where are they?" I asked excitedly, sensing things were starting to turn in Geoff Truscott's favour at last.

"Up in one of the attics in the old mansion. In a big old metal filing cabinet they used for keeping paper files in in the old days, but stopped using when we got a new system installed." He replied.

"I'd better tell Eddie where I'm going." I suddenly remembered the errant foreman, who'd promised to come back, but hadn't. "He might wonder where I am."

"Oh, didn't I tell you?" My companion struck the side of his hand with his hand. "He's gone home. Left us to do the locking up tonight."

"Typical!" I laughed. "Come on then, Mr Montgomery, you lead the way!" I turned the lights off and followed in his wake towards the mansion, and the new evidence of Geoff Truscott's innocence, I hoped we'd find there.

CHAPTER SIXTEEN

I stood on the roof of the mansion looking out towards Wales. I was bored. I couldn't see why Mr Montgomery had suggested we went up there to look through files which had proved to have nothing of value for us in them at all. Just a few old bits of correspondence. Dating back to the period when Geoff Truscott had worked at Moorecroft House admittedly, but containing nothing of note. Just a letter or two about things which had been bought at the time and one which referred to a fete they were going to hold in the summer. It seemed almost as if anything of note, which might lead us to who had really killed Frances and her husband, had been cleared away. Shredded probably. Even so, there was something I had seen amongst them which was nagging at me now for some reason I couldn't quite get to grips with. If only I could figure out what it was that was bugging me I felt the mystery of who had really done the murders would suddenly become clear. I couldn't quite put my finger on what it was in the old correspondence that was troubling me, though, and that was why I had come out onto the roof to look at the view, and left Mr Montgomery to carry on alone, looking through the papers I knew were not going to be of any value to us.

It certainly was a magnificent view of the surrounding landscape I had laid out before me as I stood up here as if looking out from the ramparts of a castle. Off to the north west the highest point of the Long Mynd, the largest by far of all of the hills in the area, stood up brown and purple above the green patchwork of the Church Stretton Valley as it stretched away in front of me, carrying the railway line through All Stretton towards Shrewsbury and beyond when it did. Above the purple of the heather, the dark green of spruce trees stood out where they covered parts of the summit of the hill.

Beyond the valley, and to the north east side of it, Caer Caradoc Hill, with the remains of its hill fort, grass covered now, where the Ancient British tribal leader, Caractacus, was supposed to have made his last stand against the invading Roman army, towered away above the valley until it was hidden in the gloom.

Beyond Caradoc, and to the south east of it, the woodland-clad heights of Wenlock Edge, running from Much Wenlock in the north, to Craven Arms and beyond in the south, stood in shadow made darker by the decid-uous woodland of ash, oak and rowan, which covered its summit.

Looking to the west, though, you could see into Wales, just as men had probably stood and looked out from high points like this in that direction for centuries in the past, fearing the appearance of wild warriors sweeping in from the west, with the sole object of mov-ing the border eastward again, as they had so many times in the past. There the setting sun, still going down in Wales probably, was hidden by the heights of the Long Mynd.

To the south west, more of the Church Stretton Val-ley ran down towards Craven Arms, with more of Wenlock Edge towering above it, and Round Hill, Wart Hill and the steep scarps of Hopesay Hill too. Countless bogs, mosses and grasses were hidden in the shadows of the higher hilltops, which rose up above the lower areas and could be seen as high points of land in the distance.

I was looking that way now when the realization of what it was had been bugging me suddenly struck me with a force which took my breath away. It was the spelling of the name Montgomery in the signatures authorising many of the letters and other correspondence over the years. The name of the man I had left sorting through the old files he must have known wouldn't reveal any secrets concerning the true perpetrator of The House of Horror Hammer Murders. P Montgomery! P for Phil perhaps?

I felt the blood in my veins turning to ice, but knew I had to go back inside. Back to those dusty old files. Look again to verify my discovery, and either put my mind at rest, or frighten myself to death, but without giving my companion any hint of the fear of him suddenly welling up inside me as I did so.

But in that I was already too late, it seemed. Something I had done must have given some sign of my excitement, because I could suddenly sense my companion standing close behind me on the edge of the roof. I knew, without being able to see him, that he was looking at me strangely. As if he could read my mind. And in that same instant I was only too painfully aware of the vulnerability of my position. After all, I was alone up here, after everyone else had gone home, with a man who may have already killed two people by striking them repeatedly on the head with a hammer, and the thought had obviously occurred to my companion too, because I turned and caught him watching me covertly out of the corner of his eye.

Knowing I had nothing to lose now by laying my cards firmly on the table, I bit the bullet, and faced him challengingly. "It was *you* wasn't it?" I said, hoping the tremble in my voice wouldn't warn him of the fear I was feeling in my heart. "Not Geoff Truscott."

"What was me?" He stared down at me challengingly from his greater height.

"You who killed Frances and her husband." I answered, as if it was the most natural thing for me to be saying to the man.

"That's a very dangerous accusation for someone to be making," he took a threatening step towards me, looking me firmly in the eyes, and holding my gaze with his. "Someone with no way of proving it."

"Anyone who'd ever spoken to Geoff Truscott would know he wasn't capable of anything so brutal and so callous. I can't see why people believed it at the time." I stood my ground and returned his gaze, hoping he wouldn't notice the tremble which now took in my whole body, because I was desperately frightened of what might happen as a result of the can of worms I was opening here.

"Anyone who'd ever….!" He laughed out loud at that. "Listen to yourself. To what you're saying boy. You can't have ever spoken to Geoff Truscott."

"Because he's been dead for thirty years?" I asked.

"Because he's been dead for thirty years." He agreed.

"It *is* true though isn't it?" I refused to be diverted by a minor detail like that. "That he was framed for two murders he didn't commit?"

"Two murders he didn't commit, you say." Montgomery drew himself up to his full height and towered above me. Emphasising his superiority over me in every way by his actions. "Well if *he* didn't commit them, who do you reckon did? And think hard before you answer that question, boy."

"I don't *have* to think hard." I had little choice but to stand my ground and return his look, stare for stare, having well and truly burned my boats on Geoff Truscott's behalf. "There was only one other person it *could* have been, who had both motive and opportunity, and who Geoff, in all his innocence, would never ever have suspected - his friend Phil."

"Who we can't find!" He said triumphantly.

"Who *you* said you didn't know what had become of." I corrected him.

"And what's wrong with that?" He continued to look down at me. "It was all a very long time ago. A *very* long time ago. Only natural that I wouldn't know what had become of him after all this time. That was why we came up here to look through the old files, wasn't it? It's just a pity we were wasting our time in doing it, because they have revealed precisely nothing about the identity of this mysterious fellow, Phil."

"Not *quite* nothing, Mr Montgomery," I said quietly. "Mr *P* Montgomery, according to the letters you'd signed amongst the old correspondence here. P for Philip is it? *You* were Geoff's friend Phil, weren't you? Poor innocent Geoff, who thought warning you off of seeing Frances would be enough. In fact it made you all the more determined to have her, didn't it? To add *her* scalp to the tally of married women you've been to bed with. Probably getting her away from Geoff, as well as away from her husband, was a double whammy for you, so to speak – made her conquest all the more exciting in your eyes. Poor Geoff!"

"Poor Geoff be damned! He was so far out of his league with that one it was an affront to me to see them together every day."

"So you wheedled your way into Frances's affections, got her hooked on the drugs you were supplying her with and.....Why?" I looked at him scathingly. "Why would Frances prefer you to.....Why would any woman?"

"I gave them what they wanted," he smiled complacently, and I would have gladly pushed that smile back through his teeth if I could have, but couldn't, so said instead.

"*What*? Put a hammer through their heads?"

He adopted a tour guide stance, holding his lapels as if I was one of a group of visitors he was showing round. "If I have to. If that's what's called for."

"You admit it then?" I challenged him.

"What's to admit?" He laughed unconcernedly. "What's to deny? Who are you going to tell? Your ghostly friend?"

"I could go to the police," I said, a little nonplussed by his devil-may-care attitude.

"And tell them what the spirits told you? They'll laugh you out of the place!" And he laughed out loud himself.

"They might not, if I tell them what Geoff told me." I didn't really believe it myself, and I could see that he definitely didn't.

"They didn't believe what he said when he was alive, did they?" He chuckled to himself again. "That was why they took my version of events over his."

"But Geoff let you get away with it, because he didn't want to stay living after what you'd done to Frances. He didn't *try* to put his point across, like I'm going to now."

"They'll still laugh *you* out of the place like they did Geoff, when he finally woke up and tried to save himself. He was always an innocent adrift in the real world, him. Unable to believe that anyone could be as bad as most people *are*, if you give them the chance to be, and they think they can get away with it.

Because he'd warned Frances about me, he thought she'd do as he wanted and avoid me. It never occurred to him, that she was more like me than like him once he'd got her started her on the downward path so to speak, and she would do just what I warned him she'd do a long, long time ago. Turn to me for the extra excitement she needed, and which I could provide for her in all sorts of ways, once he'd begun to get so boring and predictable to her.

Her finding her way to me was the start of a period of her life as filled with sex, drugs, and more sex for her, as the previous months with Geoff had been devoid of it.

Every evening that she was meeting me, she'd hurry home, cook herself and that gormless frog husband of hers something to eat which didn't have too many calories in it, so it wouldn't slow her down at all, then she'd wash and change, and be back here around eight o'clock, when everyone else had gone home. Three or four hours later, we'd stagger out to our cars, and drive blearily home for the few hours sleep, which were all we could fit in before it was time to be getting up, and back here again for the next morning's work."

He smiled complacently, and I took the opportunity to interrupt his story with a question. "You came back *here*?"

"Yes. Most nights. Why?"

"I thought you always went to *her* house. I thought that was where you were when her husband burst in on you."

"No. She was funny that way. Didn't mind betraying her husband here, on the sofa, but not in the marital bed. Somehow, in *her* mind, that would have made the whole thing much worse."

"How did he catch you together then?" I interrupted, picking him up on something which didn't quite tally with what had been said in court. "Did he come here looking for her?"

Montgomery glared at my impudence in speaking, obviously not used to being stopped short when he was in full flow. "He didn't." He said with a frown.

"Didn't what?"

"Didn't catch us together. It was Mary who did that. The nosy cow!" His frown grew stronger at the memory. Someone else who hadn't let him have it all his own way, it seemed.

"Mary *who*?" I was getting really out of my depth now. Finding *his* account of events as difficult to follow as any of Geoff Truscott's stories had been.

"Mary Hendry, a rough looking woman about the same age as Frances, who used to work in the office here. Had an idea something was going on at night that

189

shouldn't be, after I'd had Frances across her desk one night, by way of a change.

Something can't have been put back right afterwards, or something left behind, I don't know what. Just know she started to nose about after that. And one night she came back and caught us together on the sofa, when we'd just got dressed again after going away at each other like a couple of rabbits. Frances was just saying we couldn't go on the way we were, but reaching out for me again just the same. And I was just breathing into her ear that we could keep going that way as long as we kept taking the tablets, when fat Mary sidled into the room, and stood looking down at us with a look of such triumph on her face, like she'd just won the lottery or something. "Frances! Philip!" She cooed. "Fancy you both being here!"

Just fancy! I waited to take my lead from Frances, who had sprung to the opposite end of the sofa from me, as if she had been stung, and now seemed intent on treating me as if I was one step short of a total stranger, without going any way towards fooling bloody Mary Hendry. That woman, I was sure, knew *exactly* what we were about. The way she was watching me was too obvious for her not to have known just how many times I'd been on that sofa with Frances before, but I had the feeling she would have happily swapped places with Frances if she could have done, and be damned to her own husband. We passed a very uncomfortable hour or so before she finally went home.

The quarrel broke the instant the door had finally closed behind her. It was heated, vicious, and brief. Bloody Mary Hendry catching us together like that had brought Frances face to face with the part she felt she was playing. Brought into the open the guilt she felt, but had been carefully holding down inside her, over the way she'd been betraying her husband. "I mean," she said, all guilty all of a sudden because we'd been caught out, "it can't be very real for me to have been doing what I've been doing these past few weeks. I don't know what possessed me to be here with you. I don't know what Mary must think."

"Does it matter what she thinks?" I said, because, to my mind, it didn't. Frances obviously saw it very differently, though.

"That's always your answer isn't it?" She snapped. "Does it matter what this or that person thinks? Well yes, it does, actually. To me anyway! And to you as well, if you really cared as much for me as you're always pretending you do. I love my husband! I refuse to have anyone think I don't. Now please go."

I got to my feet very slowly. Not prepared to let her end it just like that. I mean, who did the woman think she was? Telling *me* to go!

She'd been moving around the room as we argued. First sitting on the arm of a chair, then standing fingering football magazines in a rack. Now, she stood looking at me with a look almost of hate on her face.

"Frances I...." I set off on one final attempt to deflect her from what she thought she was going to do. To make her come back to me, so I could finish the affair at a time that was of *my* choosing, not hers. Putting my arms around her waist, I tried to pull her to me and smother her with kisses, but she wouldn't let me.

"I want you to go!" She said, trying to push me away, but I wasn't having *that*. Not from *her*! Not from *any* woman! I pushed back and we struggled for a minute and then, and I really don't know how it happened, she was on the ground, with her head on the hearth, and there was blood everywhere.

"You killed her *here*?" I broke in as he stopped talking.

"I killed her *here*." He agreed, stony faced.

"Then how…..?" I started to ask, but he interrupted.

"How did her body come to be at her house?"

"Yes."

"I took it there in my car. After cleaning the blood off the hearth with a towel, I wrapped her up in a blanket I had in the boot and carried her into the house and laid her out on her bed."

"Why?"

"I can't really answer that." He said slowly, as if reliving the moment. "Because I simply don't know. It's all too long ago now to remember the details. I think I was still trying to cover up what had happened in the rest room."

"Despite Mary Hendry? I asked.

"Despite Mary Hendry." He agreed.

"But how did Jean, Frances's husband, get involved?"

"Came home unexpectedly." Montgomery shook his head at the memory. "He was supposed to be away for the week, at a conference of hoteliers, or something, that was why I thought I could get away with taking her body there. Instead, he came home whilst I was arranging things in the bedroom, attacked me with a hammer and……"

"And after that it was pretty much as reported in the press?" I stopped him there. Not really wanting to hear the grisly details from the real murderer's lips.

"Pretty much." He agreed soberly.

"What about Mary Hendry?" I asked.

"What *about* her?" He asked back.

"Didn't she go to the police and tell them about seeing you here with Frances the night before?"

"Why should she?" Montgomery seemed surprised at the question.

"To save Geoff of course."

"Why would she want to save Geoff at *my* expense?" He laughed at the thought. "No one here liked Geoff very much. He was too serious about things. Besides, I saw her alright, had sex with her whenever she wanted, and told her how Geoff had been fucking Frances too, but she'd got tired of him, so he'd killed her."

"And she believed you?"

"Yes, why shouldn't she? She'd always fancied me," I could have cheerfully rammed the self-satisfied smile he had on his face as he said that, down his throat if I'd been able, "but, like everyone else, she didn't have much time for Geoff."

"Poor Geoff!"

"Poor Geoff be damned! He shouldn't have tried to score with someone as way out of his league as Frances was! Love of *his* life she might have been, but *he* was never that for *her*."

"And I suppose you think *you* were?"

"I'm *sure* I was," he said complacently. "But she was never anything more than just a passing grind to me."

"Poor Geoff!" I said. "Poor Frances! You can't be allowed to get away with this, you know. Whatever they say to me when I do it, I *am* going to the police."

"Don't you threaten *me* boy!" He came closer, towering above me as I stood there defiantly. "You're in a very vulnerable position there, you know."

"Someone would be bound to suspect foul play if you were involved in a second murder." I hoped I sounded more convincing than I felt.

"Ah, but then, you see, I was never *involved* in the first one, other than as the informant who steered the police towards Geoff, and he was perfect as a fall guy. No resistance. No reason to live once he'd lost his precious Frances! I planted the evidence in his locker, then tipped off the police where to find it, and on the way had a long chat with a policeman who wanted to make a name for himself and had no interest in ethics, telling him about Geoff's drug habit and excessive sexual demands. A perfect crime, even if I say so myself."

"Until Geoff came back from the dead and told me the alternative story I'm going to be telling the police when I go to see them later."

He moved a step closer still and I could feel my heels overlapping the top stair. "If I was to push you down those stairs, which look so invitingly close behind you, you'd fall right down through the building and would be bound to break something vital by the time you hit the floor in the basement. If I really thought you were going to squeal on me, or they were likely to believe you if you did, that would be what I'd have to do to shut you up, just like I did the others."

"But then you'd have to do it to me too," a voice said softly from behind him, "and that might not be so easy."

"Eddie!" I looked beyond my would-be assailant. Then pushed past him, so I could stand next to the balding foreman, away from the dangerous top step I'd been teetering on. Never had I been as pleased to see *anyone*, as I had been when I saw Eddie Ponting standing there. "I thought you'd gone home!"

"That was what I wanted you to think. Or what I wanted Montgomery to think. I've never trusted him since Annie, the girl who worked here before you, told me what he'd suggested they do together. And her pregnant too! She didn't want to make a fuss about it, because she was leaving anyway, but it made me mark his card for him.

When he seemed in such an all-fired hurry to get you to go up into the attics with him, and for me to go home early, I began to wonder if he was ambidextrous in sexual matters, liked a bit either way, so to speak, so I let him think I'd gone home early and followed on behind.

I was expecting him to try to get up to some sort of hanky panky with you, but not this! Not another murder."

"*Another* murder?" Montgomery tried, without success, to maintain his act of bravado. "What do you mean, *another* murder?"

"I was standing there for quite a while listening." Eddie replied. "I heard you admitting to – no boasting about – killing Frances and Jean Delamore, and planting evidence in Geoff Truscott's locker, so the police would think *he'd* done it. I think you've done for yourself this time mister, because I heard *that* from your own lips. It's no longer a case of a young lad trying to get the police to believe something he said he was told by as ghost. I heard *that* boast from you."

"They won't believe it!" Montgomery blustered, moving closer to Eddie, bringing his greater height into play, and trying to stare him down.

"I think they will." Eddie stood his ground, refusing to give an inch, as the two stood toe to toe, looking threateningly into each other's eyes. "What reason have *I* got to lie? It's just a pity that, though someone else was topped for what you did, that can't happen to *you* now. They should bring back capital punishment just for you!"

Montgomery backed away from Eddie for a moment, then there was suddenly a knife in his hand, and he was aiming it at Eddie's stomach, but something, I couldn't make out what, but it felt like a wind blowing strongly enough as it passed us, to topple the filing cabinet over with such force, that it struck Montgomery as he lunged at Eddie, and sent him tumbling through a hole which had opened up in the floor of the attic, then down the stairs he'd been threatening to push me down only minutes earlier. He hit the floor in the basement with a bone-grinding crunch, followed swiftly by the filing cabinet, which had travelled with such speed it must have squashed him flat when it landed on him. Above it all, moving at such speed himself I could never be sure of it when I was telling the story later, but seemingly directing the way things fell, so they fell *as* they did, in the order they did, swept an avenging angel in the form of Geoff Truscott.

CHAPTER SEVENTEEN

Of course, the official version of events was, that a combination of death watch beetle and dry rot in the roof area, had served to render the floorboards up there very thin and brittle in places, and *that*, coupled with the three of us struggling with each other around the filing cabinet, which was too heavy really to have been up there in the first place, had caused the floor to give way, with such disastrous results for Montgomery.

To my mind, that goes no way to explaining how his much lighter body, having gone through the hole first, fell much faster than the heavy filing cabinet, which eventually landed on top of him and crushed him to death. But I have to concede that Eddie did tell me privately that he was sorry, but he hadn't seen Geoff up there at all. Mind, Eddie had never seen Geoff when he'd been wandering the gardens either, but then I suppose there was only *me* who actually had. Besides, I had to forgive Eddie for not really believing that I had ever seen Geoff, because it was thanks to his testimony, which didn't include any evidence given by ghosts, just that which he had heard Montgomery confessing to with his own lips, namely the murders of Frances and Jean Delamore, and the manipulation of the evidence to frame Geoff Truscott, that the latter had to be given a posthumous pardon for his execution for murder and the investigation of the police officers who had knowingly gone along with the manipulation was still ongoing. Giving more power to the elbows of the anti-bring-back-hanging brigade.

In fighting the case for a pardon for Geoff, the lawyers instructed to handle things on his behalf, paid for by the Delamore family of France, it was rumoured, but never confirmed, who wanted to see justice done on behalf of their son, and the true murderer named, even if he had gone beyond justice in this life, made much of the many similarities his case had with the case of Timothy Evans, who was executed for two murders in 1950, then pardoned in 1965, when it was decided it was more likely that Harold Christie, the infamous serial murderer, had committed the murders.

In *both* cases, the Delamore's lawyers, if they *were* the Delamore's lawyers, *maintained*, there were two murders and in *both* cases, the true murderer had given evidence against the person wrongly convicted, ie Harold Christie in the case of Timothy Evans, and Philip Montgomery in the case of Geoff Truscott.

Timothy Evans had been put on trial for the murder of his daughter on 11th January 1950, having confessed to the murders in the beginning- something which Geoff Truscott had never done in regard to the murders *he* was accused of - but then recanted his confession during consultations with his solicitor. Alleging after that, that Christie had always been responsible for the murders. This was the basis of Evans's defence in his trial, which he maintained was the truth until his execution. Subsequent events were to confirm the veracity of Evans's claims.

Christie, the real murderer, was a key witness for the prosecution, just as Philip Montgomery had been a key witness for the prosecution of Geoff Truscott. Christie denied that he had offered to abort Beryl Evan's unborn child, and gave detailed evidence about the quarrels between Evans and his wife. The defence sought to show how Christie was the murderer, by highlighting his past criminal record.

Christie had previous convictions for several thefts and malicious wounding. But his apparent reformation, and his service with the police, impressed the jury. The defence could not find a motive for why a supposedly respectable person like Christie would want to murder two people. The prosecution, on the other hand, could use the explanation in Evans's confessions, as Evans's motive for wanting to kill the victims, despite Evans having no criminal record.

In Geoff's case, there *was* no defence, so no need for his lawyer to try to down Montgomery's reputation in any way. *That* was, in any case, as far as anyone who didn't know him well was concerned, spotless, but had they conducted a thorough search of Montgomery's house, they must surely have found some evidence of drugs usage at least. And *that* ought to have made them wonder about the drugs they had found in Geoff's locker.

In the same way, had the police conducted a thorough search of Christie's garden, and found the bones of two prior victims which he had buried there, Evan's trial might not have happened at all, and a serial killer would have been prevented from murdering again. Evans's reputation for conflicting statements fatally undermined his credibility, however.

That reputation, was created by the police themselves, in preparing several false confessions, just as the police in the case of the House of Horror Hammer Murders, had accepted, without question, whatever they had been told by Philip Montgomery, the *real* murderer, whilst undermining the credibility of the totally innocent Geoff Truscott, by making him out to be practically a recluse, with no friends at all.

During Evan's trial, things by and large, came down to a case of Christie's word against Evans's, just as in Geoff's, it was largely a case of Montgomery's word against *his*. He *wasn't* given the benefit of knowing who it was had given testimony against him, though. That remained secret throughout the trial.

Geoff's trial, like Timothy Evans trial, lasted only three days, and much key evidence was omitted, or never shown to the jury. The judge was prejudiced against Evans from the start, just as the judge in Geoff's case seemed to be prejudiced against *him*, and his summing-up biased against the defendant. Timothy Evans was found guilty, and hanged on 9th March 1950. Geoff Truscott was hanged on 19th June 1963.

The safety of Evans's conviction was severely criticised when Christie's murders were discovered three years later. During interviews with police and psychiatrists prior to his execution, Christie admitted several times that he had been responsible for the murder of Beryl Evans. If these confessions were true, Evans's second statement detailing Christie's offer to abort Beryl's baby is the true version of events that took place in Rillington Place on 8th November 1949.

In 1955, a delegation was formed to petition the Home Secretary for a new inquiry, because of people's dissatisfaction with the conclusions of the Scott Henderson Inquiry. But nothing much happened until 1965, when the then Home Secretary ordered a new inquiry, which found it was "more probable than not" that Evans murdered his wife, but that he did not murder his daughter.

This was entirely contrary to the prosecution case in Evans's trial, which had held that both murders had been committed by the same person, as a single transaction. The victims' bodies had been found together in the same location and had been murdered in the same way by strangulation.

Despite this conclusion, the enquiry *did* expose police malpractice during the Evans case, such as destruction of evidence. The tie which had been used to strangle Geraldine, for example, was destroyed by the police prior to the discovery of Christie's crimes in 1953, just as evidence against Montgomery, linking him with the House of Horror Hammer Murders, seemed to have been destroyed in *his* case. Even the record book, in which the destruction had to be noted, was itself destroyed by the police. In most serious cases, police are required to preserve all material and documentary evidence, so the removal of evidence in Geoff's case was, in itself, suspicious. Many police statements were contradictory and confused as to dates and times of interviews with key witnesses, especially of the Christies during the first murder case. The judge went to great lengths to prefer police evidence wherever possible, and exonerate them of any police misconduct (such as threats of violence against Evans during his interrogation), and he didn't address the allegations about the validity of several of the confessions allegedly made by Evans. He never considered the incompetence of the police in their searches of the garden at Rillington Place, and had a poor under-standing of the importance of forensic evidence. The enquiry did little to settle the many issues which arose from the case, but, by exonerating Evans of killing his child, was crucial in subsequent events.

Since Evans had only been convicted of the murder of his daughter, the Home Secretary recommended a royal pardon for Evans, which was granted in October 1966. In 1965 Evans' remains had been exhumed from Pentonville Prison and reburied in St Patrick's Roman Catholic Cemetery in Leytonstone, Greater London. The outcry over the Evans case contributed, first to the suspension, and then to the abolition, of capital punishment in Great Britain. Too late for Geoff Truscott, who had been executed for the murders he didn't commit three years before that. A strange anomaly of what had happened to him being that it had only been because he was able to come back as a ghost and start the ball rolling through me confronting Montgomery, the real murderer, that his innocence had been able to be proved. Had he not been executed, he would not have been able to do that, but would have been just one more innocent man in prison for a crime he didn't commit, but which nobody else believed he didn't commit.

Once the more important business of proving Geoff's innocence was out of the way, I began to spend most of my spare time looking into the legend of the Grey Lady said to haunt the grounds of Moorecroft House, to see if there could be any basis for the story, despite having been told it was only made up in the first place to draw in the punters, and did eventually arrive at an account of the various happenings connected with the

Grey Lady, which drew in Geoff Truscott. All of which *did* point to the likelihood that the haunted track really *was* a haunted track, which had been haunted for a long time. And not just by Geoff Truscott either. The hauntings dated back beyond the first involvement of the Moorecroft family in the gardens, when their family's name had still been de la More.

The de la More family had risen to prominence in France, and more especially in Normandy, sometime during the ninth century. When their fellow Normans, under the leadership of Duke William of Normandy, had invaded England in 1066, they had joined in too, throwing in their lot with the family who were their Signeurs in France. The Montgomeries.

Roger de Montgomerie, Signeur of Montgomerie, was a relative, probably a grandnephew, of the Duchess Gunnor, wife of Duke Richard 1 of Normandy, father of William the Conqueror. He had large holdings in central Normandy, chiefly in the valley of the Dives, and these his son, another Roger, inherited.

That Roger was one of William the Conqueror's principal counsellors, and commanded the Norman right flank at Hastings, returning to Normandy with King William in 1067, after which he was entrusted with a great deal of land in England to reward him for his support. Eighty-three manors in Sussex; seven-eighths of Shropshire, including the earldom of Shrewsbury; estates amounting to four manors in Surrey; nine manors in Hampshire; three manors in Wiltshire; eight manors in Middlesex; one manor in Gloucestershire; two manors in Worcestershire; eight manors in Cambridgeshire; eleven manors in Warwickshire; and thirty manors in Stafford-shire.

After William I's death in 1087, Roger Montgomery joined with other rebels to overthrow the newly crowned King William II in the Rebellion of 1088. William, however, was able to convince Roger to abandon the rebellion and side with him. This worked out favourably for Roger, as the rebels were beaten and lost their land holdings in England.

By then Roger had married his first wife, Mabel de Belleme, who was heiress to a large territory on both sides of the border between Normandy and Maine in France, and by whom he had 10 children: Hugh of Montgomery, 2nd Earl of Shrewsbury, who died child-less in 1098; Roger de Belleme Count of Alençon, who, in 1082, succeeded his younger brother Hugh and be-came 3rd Earl of Shrewsbury, married Agnes, Countess of Ponthieu and died in 1131; Roger the Poitevin, Vicomte d'Hiemois, who married Adelmode de la Marche; Philip of Montgomery; Arnulf of Montgomery, who married Lafracota, daughter of Muirchertach Ua Briain; Sibyl of Montgomery, who married Robert Fitzhamon, Lord of Creully; Emma, abbess of Almencheches; Matilda (Maud) of Montgomery, who married Robert, Count of Mortain, and died around 1085; Mabel of Montgomery, who married Hugh de Châteauneuf; Roger of Montgomery, who died young.

After Mabel's death in 1077 Roger, by now First Earl of Shrewsbury, married Adelaide de Le Puiset, by whom he had one son, Everard, who entered the Church.

After Roger's death, his estates were divided. His eldest surviving son, Robert, received the bulk of the

Norman estates (as well as his mother's estates), whilst the next son, Hugh, received the bulk of the English estates and the Earldom of Shrewsbury. After Hugh's death *his* eldest son, another Robert, inherited the earldom.

Jean de la More, the first of that name to live in England, had fought at the Battle of Hastings in the vanguard of the knights supporting the Roger Montgomery who had come to England with William the Conqueror and become the First Earl of Shrewsbury. Because of his support of Roger during the Norman Conquest and after, he was given extensive lands in Shropshire as a reward.

Amongst these lands was an area of moorland on the hills behind Church Stretton, beyond Ashbrook, where the Cardingmill Valley meets the town, and which Jean de la More was particularly taken with as soon as he set eyes on it. Not just because of its hilltop position, which reminded him of the moorlands surrounding his family's castle in back in Normandy, and which meant that whoever was living there had a commanding view over the surrounding lands, but also because of the beauty of its aspect, and of the beauty of the manor house which was already standing there when he first saw it. He immediately chose it to be the site of what was to be his main home in England, pulled down the manor house which was already in situ, despite the protestations of the man who owned it when he first saw it, then built a castle on the same site, which eventually became a fortified manor house, and was given the family name of de la More. Later anglicised to Moorecroft.

The land de la More was so taken with was on the edge of an area of upland dotted with ancient tumuli, stone circles, and sacred wells, linked by prehistoric tracks such as The Portway, which ran the length of the Long Mynd, and the Cross Dyke, which ran from Much Wenlock to Rattlinghope and beyond. It originally had the Celtic name, Caer Cythraul, which translated as Fortress of the Devil, and was a place which anyone who had ever lived in the region, from prehistoric times onwards, had gone out of their way to avoid, even though it was so pleasing to the eye, because the track which ran across the centre of it was said to be an ancient spirit way, or corpse path, which had, in the most ancient of times, been used as a route along which dead bodies were carried to sacred sites further in the hills, to be laid out so their bones could be picked clean prior to burial.

Because so many dead bodies had been transported along the track in this way over many centuries, the path was said to have been haunted by something, or *somethings,* since those earliest times. Though by what no one would, or could, say. The Celts who moved into the area after driving the original inhabitants out, gave the hill its name, and though they set up home on nearby Caer Caradoc, they never tried living on Caer Cythraul. And when the Romans moved in to drive the Celts out of the region, though the road they built to take them to their cities in the north of England passed close by Caer Caradoc, they too kept their distance from Caer Cythraul.

The Saxons, who swept through the area after the Romans left, weren't given to respecting or worrying overmuch about earlier people's burial sites, places of worship, or the superstitions surrounding them, and may not even have been aware of the existence of the haunted track everyone had been avoiding until then. The Celts they had usurped obviously didn't bother to warn them, because the invaders apparently liked the high point on the edge of the moors so well they settled on it, and built themselves a manor there. A manor with a house which was bisected by the very line taken by the ancient corpse path. A manor which, by the time of the Norman Conquest, was in the possession of a Saxon Theign called Gunwald.

Gunwald was the last of his family. It was said that they had been a very unlucky family, who had died out quickly, in a few generations, once they had set up home where they did. The principal misfortune they suffered being a tendency for family members to kill one another even more frequently than was usual amongst Saxon families, who were very warlike at the best of times. Those who came into direct ownership of the manor were so often slain by close relatives who wanted it for themselves, one of their bards had written a ballad about it. Gunwald didn't have any close relatives left who might want to kill him, but he *did* have a home in a spot coveted by a Norman knight who had been given all rights to it by the Earl of Shrewsbury for services rendered, and he *did* have a beautiful and desirable daughter, Oswalda, who Jean de la More hoped would one day render certain services for *him*. When Gunwald refused to give in to any of these demands, de la More had his men take him further up onto the moors and kill him. Gunwald's body was never found. The girl fled into the wilderness and was never seen again either.

Jean de la More lost no time in having Gunwald's manor house pulled down and a small castle built in exactly the same spot, so it enjoyed the same commanding outlook across the country. Unfortunately for the de la Mores, it was bisected by the spirit path in just the same way. And though they didn't suffer exactly the same bad luck as the Saxons had, it became noticeable that after every three generations or so, the Lord of the Manor would have a wife who would betray him, leaving him with illegitimate sons. They didn't write ballads about it, because the Normans weren't as given to that sort of thing as the Saxons had been. But they *did* have to keep executing their wives, because of their infidelity with members of the lower classes.

The first Jean de la More's wife, Frances, did, indeed, betray him with an unnamed servant of Sir Philip Montgomery, an illegitimate son of Roger, who had been trying to have his way with the Lady himself, and who betrayed the couple to Lord de la More when he found out his own attempts at seduction had come to nought. After her dalliance with the servant, there was nothing her husband could do with Frances de la More but have her executed. Both because of her betrayal of him and their wedding vows, and so the family's bloodline wouldn't be contaminated by her actions.

By 1547, the de la More family name had been anglicised into Moorecroft and John, the first Lord of that name, had a wife, Frances, who was the Grey Lady said to haunt the grounds of Moorecroft House as a result of being executed for betraying her husband with a troubadour he had employed to play for her, but who she had taken as a lover. The couple were betrayed by Sir Philip Montgomery, a descendant of the first betrayer, after Frances Moorecroft had rejected *his* advances in favour of those of the musician.

In 1686, the then, Lady Frances Moorecroft, betrayed her husband, John, Lord Moorecroft, with a catholic priest she was hiding from the authorities in a secret room, which served as a priest's hole, and was behind moveable panelling in the library.

Whether the couple had only been engaged in the, then, capital crime of being practicing Catholics, or they had taken things further, as the man who betrayed them – Sir Philip Montgomery, a close friend of Lord Moorecroft – claimed, and the unnamed priest, who was supposed to be celibate, had betrayed his religion for Lady Moorecroft, whilst she had betrayed both her husband *and* her religion, by having an affair with the priest, isn't certain. It was rumoured at the time, that Sir Philip had only given away the couple's relationship, and the priest's presence in the house, when Lady Frances had refused to sleep with him as well.

That was the final act of betrayal the Moorecroft family had to suffer. After that the direct line of the Moorecroft's died out, probably because of so many wives having to be executed and so many sons having to be declared illegitimate. The house was then sold to a family of a different name, with no connection to the Moorecrofts at all.

When their new home was burned down in the night shortly afterwards, by what may have been a maid's accident with her night candle, or may have been a fire of a more mysterious nature, the incoming family took the decision to build their replacement house on the opposite side of the plot from where the original house had been, and probably saved their own lives, and the lives of many of their descendants, from misfortune by doing so.

That might have been the end of things as far as the ill luck suffered by those families who had lived over the haunted path was concerned but, in 1962, Frances Delamore came to work as a tour guide in the gardens of Moorecroft House. One of the routes she had to walk every day whilst showing visitors around, being along the haunted path. The one the house the Moorecroft family had built had straddled before it was burned down.

Frances' husband, Jean, was a direct descendant of the line of the Delamore family that had stayed in France when the others came to England amongst the supporters of Roger de Montgomerie, in William the Conqueror's invading army, and had retained the French version of the name. Holding on to lands in Normandy they held for William, as Duke of Normandy, they, then, transferred their allegiance to the Kings of France, when William didn't return.

Frances was a distant cousin of Jean, and her name had already been Delamore before she married him because, though her ancestors had been members of that branch of the family which had come to England with William the Conqueror, they were not amongst those who had changed their name to Moorecroft. With their marriage, the two sides of the family came together, and in so doing seemed to reawaken the power of whatever spirits it was haunted the corpse path, and had brought the Delamores and Moorecrofts such ill luck in the past.

And it drew in Geoff Truscott and Philip Montgomery too, the latter a descendant of the original players in the drama, when they also found their way to work in the gardens as tour guides. The first time there had been such a connection for hundreds of years. Making the misfortune they brought down on their heads by so doing, all the more overwhelming, and impossible for them to resist, as a result.

The reason Geoff Truscott appeared to me whist I was working in the grounds was, I believe, largely because of my family history. My grandfather table tapping for spirits, and my Aunt Maggie taking me to visit mediums, had made me more receptive than most to the spirit world, and able to accept their appearance without question, because I believed in their existence anyway. Unlike Eddie Ponting, who did not. And I had felt, even before I went to work there, that my grandfather was steering me in that direction for some reason.

Whether Geoff would have still appeared, but just not been seen by anyone, if I hadn't been there to see him, or whether it was my presence drew him there, I couldn't say, and will never know. His first appearance in the gardens coincided with mine, and both coincided with the bodies of those prisoners executed over the years at Shrewsbury prison for murder being exhumed, their bodies cremated, and their ashes scattered somewhere.

Because, whatever the prison authorities were denying in the report Montgomery had torn out of his newspaper to add to his file about the House of Horror Hammer Murders, that was what they *did* have to admit to at a later date, and was, to my way of thinking, what had happened to make Geoff's spirit appear. That was why he seemed so confused the first time I met him. Unable to keep focussed on anything for very long. His spirit had only just been freed in that way that morning and was still finding its way. It was also why he didn't know anything about Elton John or the Beatles. He wasn't being pretentious. Having been executed in 1962 before any of them were famous, he simply hadn't heard of them.

Whether the ashes had been scattered in the grounds of Moorecroft House, where Geoff Truscott had worked during his lifetime, still no one will say, but I believe that the simple fact of it happening *had* been enough to upset the equilibrium of things, and cause his spirit to walk along the haunted track. And whatever Eddie Ponting thought, it really *was* a haunted track, the one which had featured in the earliest of the legends sur-rounding the area. One which restless spirits had passed along many times before. Even if they hadn't been seen by anyone in the vicinity at the time who was tuned in enough to their presence to be aware of them, and where, by the greatest of co-incidences, someone who *was* tuned in to them – namely me - had come to work the very same day.

I'm not sure why Geoff Truscott was dressed in Elizabethan clothes as he was, though. It *could* have been for a totally different reason altogether from him being a tour guide. Because, despite what Eddie and Joe had said when talking about their own era, it *was* the practice for tour guides to dress up in costume when showing visitors around in Geoff's. The reason he was dressed as he was, *could* have been a connection with the troubadour executed along with the first Lady Moore-croft after they had been caught in bed together, howev-er. One of those distant echoes of forgotten lives, Geoff had spoken to me about. In which case, the priest may well have been part of the same cycle, which would account for Geoff wearing clothes from a later era the second time he appeared, and for him to be wearing modern clothes the third time he appeared.

Perhaps when he first saw Frances in the rest room at Moorecroft House that day, and was so strongly attracted to her, it was because of the connection he sensed through all those previous lives they'd shared together, without being aware how many times he'd already died a violent death of some sort because of her. Maybe *that* was what he'd seen when he'd disappeared so suddenly that final day we were together. Not the *manner* of his death, the last time it had happened, but how many times it had already happened to him in a similar fashion. Trapped in a cycle of reliving his life over and over again, along with Frances and Jean Delamore, and Philip Montgomery, I felt Geoff, or someone like him, would have to go through the whole thing at least once more before it was all over.

Frances' spirit appearing to me the way it did was different. Because it was nothing to do with anything that had gone before. Though she was, I am sure, part of that same constantly repeating cycle Montgomery and Geoff were also a part of, the difference, on this occasion, was that, because she had been so brutally murdered in the rest room where I saw her, her ghost was the ghost of the incarnation of Frances Delamore who had worked with Geoff Truscott, and was haunting there and nowhere else. The place where she had died. She must have been there since her body was brutalised in that way. Her spirit, separated from it, hovering in the corner of the room where the murder had happened. Appearing to be dressed in the way she had been dressed when she had been killed. Not seen by anyone until I came along.

That was why she had difficulty in speaking to me at first. Difficulty in grasping the fact that I was able to see her and speak to her, when nobody else ever had. From what she said to me when I was able to get her talking, though, it seemed that, though Geoff had believed her to be the love of his life, perhaps because of their previous history together, she and he had been on a collision course all the while he was pursuing her. Though how much of that was also as a result of the histories of their past lives together I couldn't say.

It was obvious, too, that she believed she had the good looks and charisma to get any man to do whatever she wanted. Just as all the other Frances Delamores down through the ages probably had as well.

In this instance though, from what Philip Montgomery had revealed to me in his boasting about her, when we'd been up on the roof together, things weren't quite the same as they had been in the past. Perhaps they never were always *exactly* the same. Perhaps variances from the previous times crept in on every occasion. On this occasion it was obvious she had been overconfident about her charms, and had fallen down just as Montgomery had told Geoff she would. Probably more as a result of her over reliance on drugs this time, than for any other failing on her part.

It had been because of my previous experience with contacting ghosts, thanks to my Grandfather and my Aunt Maggie, that I had been able to speak to Frances in the way that I had. It was also thanks to Aunt Maggie that I was eventually able to find someone who would come and talk to Frances and help her spirit to find peace and move on, so it would no longer be tied to that room.

Frances' spirit had been tied to the spot where she had been murdered in life. Geoff's spirit had more freedom to move about, once it was freed by his body being dug up and cremated in the way that it had been, but seemed, nonetheless, to be tied to the haunted track. Not just because it really *was* a haunted track, with a very long association with dead bodies and death, but because the associations Geoff and Frances had had with the track in all their lives together, not just in the life they'd most recently shared, had drawn him, at least, back to it in death. Even though she couldn't join him.

And because she couldn't, it was only with someone like me, who could see them and communicate with them both, as I was able to do, that they could make contact in any way. And, whatever people believed about the truth of their story and its outcome, my answer to the doubters has always been that I must have been able to see Geoff and Frances and speak to Geoff and Frances, or how else could we have arrived at the point where I could clear his name? And that was something I was glad I was able to do...
....
......"Do you think Frances Delamore *has* found peace now? And Geoff Truscott too?"

"I like to think so, but how will we know?"

"If the cycle's been broken it would point to it, wouldn't it?"

"Yes, but as I say, we'll only know that if the curse never affects anyone again. And it could be centuries in the future before we can say that for certain."

I looked across the tour guides rest room at the woman who had asked the questions. Tall, blonde, American. About twenty five or so years old I would have hazarded. So quite a bit younger than me. She'd been working at Moorecroft House for about three weeks now. A seasonal tour guide taken on for the summer.

I was senior tour guide now. Having changed course in my career as soon as I was able, and risen up through the ranks. Molly Lampard, *her* name was, and she'd been taken on whilst I'd been enjoying the two weeks holiday I'd just come back from, so this was the first time I'd met her. I'd been telling her the story of Geoff Truscott and Frances Delamore to while away a wet afternoon.

"It could all kick in again next week though, couldn't it?"

"I hope not Molly, because there will only be the two of us here for the next couple of weeks if it does." I said with mock seriousness. "That was why you were taken on when you were. Everyone else will be on holiday. So if it *does* start again next week, it will involve you and me."

She didn't smile at that like I'd expected her to, which was a pity, because she had a very attractive smile, I'd noticed. Sort of lop sided, and it took in her eyes. Instead, she looked at me very seriously, and seemed to be weighing something up in her mind as she did so, but she had the sort of face I found attractive when it was being serious too. Even though I shouldn't have done, really. Bearing in mind the fact that she was married, and I was her boss. Looking at her now I was reminded of someone. But couldn't quite place who.

"I think I ought to declare a personal interest in your story." She said, her careful study of me having apparently brought her to a decision about whatever it was she had been thinking over.

"A personal interest?" I looked at her in some surprise.

"Yes. I'm afraid I haven't been totally honest with any of you here."

"No?"

"No. You see, Molly isn't really my name, it's Frankie, and before I got married I was Frances Delamore Lampard. Named after my grandmother, you see?"

"Your grandmother?" I felt a sudden stab of concern. No wonder she had reminded me of someone.

"Yes. The Frances Delamore you've been telling me about."

"She can't have been your grandmother." I contradicted her uneasily. Hoping she was making it up as a joke, or something, for some reason, but sure in my mind, somehow, that she wasn't.

"She was." She insisted.

"The Frances Delamore in my story didn't have any children. She can't have been *anyone's* grandmother." been *anyone's* grandmother." I clutched desperately at a hope I knew was going to be dashed by the woman in front of me.

"She did so have children." My companion said firmly. "A daughter. Amy. My mother."

"Why didn't she or Geoff ever mention it then? And why was there no mention of it in any of the newspapers at the time?"

"Geoff didn't know anything about it. Frances came back from France because she'd got pregnant and didn't want Jean Delamore to know. He did eventually follow her to England, but she'd had her baby by then. A girl. My mother. She'd had her adopted by an American service family by the time Jean Delamore got here, and he never knew anything about it. Nor did anyone else. Frances kept it completely secret. It had been a difficult birth, though, and she was unable to have any more children because of it."

"But they *did* marry when Jean Delamore got to England?"

"Yes, and that made the child legitimate, but it was too late by then. Frances had had her adopted and the adoptive parents went back to the USA when my grandfather's service was over and she was brought up as an American, married another American, and they had me. My mother never told me anything about her origins though."

"Perhaps she didn't know what they were."

"Oh she knew right enough. My father was much older than my mother and died quite a few years ago. My mother was killed in an automobile accident last year, and whilst I was sorting through some old papers she'd left, I came across mention of who her real mother had been and what had become of her. I'd always wondered about my middle name being Delamore, and my mother had left a lot of newspaper cuttings and the like about it, you know?"

I did know. Only too well. And I was looking at this attractive American woman with totally different eyes now. Remembering that Frances and her husband had both been Delamores before she married him, and that if Amy Delamore had been a legitimate child the ill fortune, or whatever it was, which had been dogging the family through the centuries, might have missed a generation. Or had Amy being a legitimate child of the third generation changed things in some way? And what effect would giving the girl the middle name of Delamore have had?

"So you really *are* another Frances Delamore?" I asked, hoping she'd smile that attractive smile of hers again and tell me she'd just been joking, but she shook her head instead.

"I'm afraid so." She answered apologetically. "And that's not the end of it either."

"Not the end of it?"

"No." She said it with a guilty smile this time. Not half as attractive as the other one had been. "You see, my married name is Montgomery. My husband, Phil's, family arrived in the States on the Mayflower. They're a very old family indeed."

"*Philip* Montgomery?" I probed.

"Yes," she said, with a defiant toss of her head.

"And is he descended from the other Philip Montgomerys in my story?" I continued my probing. Hoping for a negative response I was afraid I wasn't going to get. "Not from the last one, obviously, but from the earlier ones?"

"I really don't know," she said, looking completely out of her depth in all of this. "I knew about my own family's history of course, that was why I came over to England, and why I took the job here when I found it was on offer. The rest of it though?" She shook her head helplessly. "All that infidelity, and so many murders and executions because of! I was brought up a Quaker. We don't go in for that sort of thing! And the part played by these Philip Montgomerys down through the ages? That was all new to me when you were telling it just now. And new to him too I should imagine. If I told him about it."

"Is he over in England with you?"

"No. I'm afraid our marriage has been going through a bad patch for quite a while now. That was why I came over here on my own. And why he stayed at home."

"You speak to him on the phone though?"

"Yes. On Skype usually."

"And will you tell him all this the next time the two of you get in touch?"

"What? That a lot of *his* ancestors may have been responsible for the violent deaths of a lot of *my* ancestors down through the centuries, because of a family curse - for want of a better name - we're still in the midst of? Bearing in mind that Phil and I are already hardly on speaking terms with each other anyway, and that he's more than three thousand miles away from me here. In my place, would *you*?"

I thought about Geoff Truscott, and what he had suffered because of the malign influences which seemed to have struck him down at every turn in all of this. And I thought of what all the others who had gone before him had suffered because of them too. And I thought of what had happened as a result of him and his Frances being left alone to mind the gardens here that first summer they spent together. Then I looked at the American woman looking back at me so earnestly, who I didn't find so attractive anymore. A woman who had just confessed to me, that she and her absent husband were currently going through problems in their marriage. And I wondered what consequences my being alone with her for the next two weeks was likely to bring down on *my* head. And what effect this latest twist in the tale of the Moorecroft family, with Frances Delamore married to Philip Montgomery, was going to have on us all.

Suddenly I was very afraid.

The End.

Now you've finished reading this story, why not try one of Brian W Taylor's other books available both as e-books and paperbacks from Amazon?

Why Weeps the Willow - The north Norfolk coast in the autumn of 1917. A restless ghost searches for a means of experiencing physical love again. A teenage girl tries to find her way through the pitfalls of her first love affair. A ruthless woman determines to hold on to her family's estates in the face of all adversity. A soldier is invalided home from the battlefields of France suffering from amnesia. Add incest, espionage and murder, then try to answer the question posed on a suicide's grave. Why Weeps the Willow?

Let Sleeping Evils Lie – a midnight vigil in a churchyard by students trying to contact a ghost said to haunt it, and some impromptu dabbling with an Ouija board in a youth club a few days later, awaken a sleeping evil it would have been better to leave undisturbed.

Murder in the Marches –   The wreckage of a millionaire's plane found crashed onto the side of a Welsh mountain. A burned out holiday cottage deep in the Welsh Marches, with the remains of a body still smouldering amongst the ashes. A mysterious package missing, first from the plane, and then from the cottage, that everyone is looking for, but no one can find. Too busy looking over their shoulders trying to see what the next guy is doing, no one is watching Chief Inspector Macdonald, but he's the one pulling the strings.

Secret Lovers No One Else Can See – Working for a local authority in 1975 England wasn't the best place to be if you were trying to hide your true sexuality. Especially if you were a boy passing yourself off as a girl, the obligatory staff medical you had to go through if you wanted to keep your job, and you did, was due, and you knew that if you went through with it your secret would be laid bare to a sniggering world.

Melody couldn't help being different from her workmates, but would any of them understand that when the secret she was so desperately trying to keep from them was revealed, or would they just be relieved that their own secrets, and every one of them had something they were trying to hide, were still safe from the blaze of publicity which enveloped hers?

Printed in Great Britain
by Amazon.co.uk, Ltd.,
Marston Gate.